Stubbed Toes & Dating Woes

HOT TREE PUBLISHING

DAHLIA DONOVAN

ALSO BY DAHLIA DONOVAN

The Grasmere Cottage Mystery Trilogy

Dead in the Garden | Dead in the Pond | Dead in the Shop

Motts Cold Case Mystery Series

Poisoned Primrose | Pierced Peony | Pickled Petunia | Purloined Poinsettia

London Podcast Mystery Series

Cosplay Killer | Ghost Light Killer | Crown Court Killer

Stand-alone Romances

After the Scrum | At War With A Broken Heart | Forged in Flood | Found You | By the Fire | One Last Heist | Pure Dumb Luck | Here Comes The Son | All Lathered Up | Not Even A Mouse | Farm to Fabre | The Misguided Confession

The Sin Bin (Complete Series)

The Wanderer | The Caretaker | The Royal Marine | The Botanist | The Unexpected Santa | The Lion Tamer | Haka Ever After | Complete Box Set

For information, contact the publisher, Hot Tree Publishing.

WWW.HOTTREEPUBLISHING.COM

EDITING: HOT TREE EDITING

COVER DESIGNER: BOOKSSMITH DESIGN

E-BOOK ISBN: 978-1-922679-58-1

PAPERBACK ISBN: 978-1-922679-60-4

STUBBED TOES & DATING WOES

DAHLIA DONOVAN

HOT TREE PUBLISHING

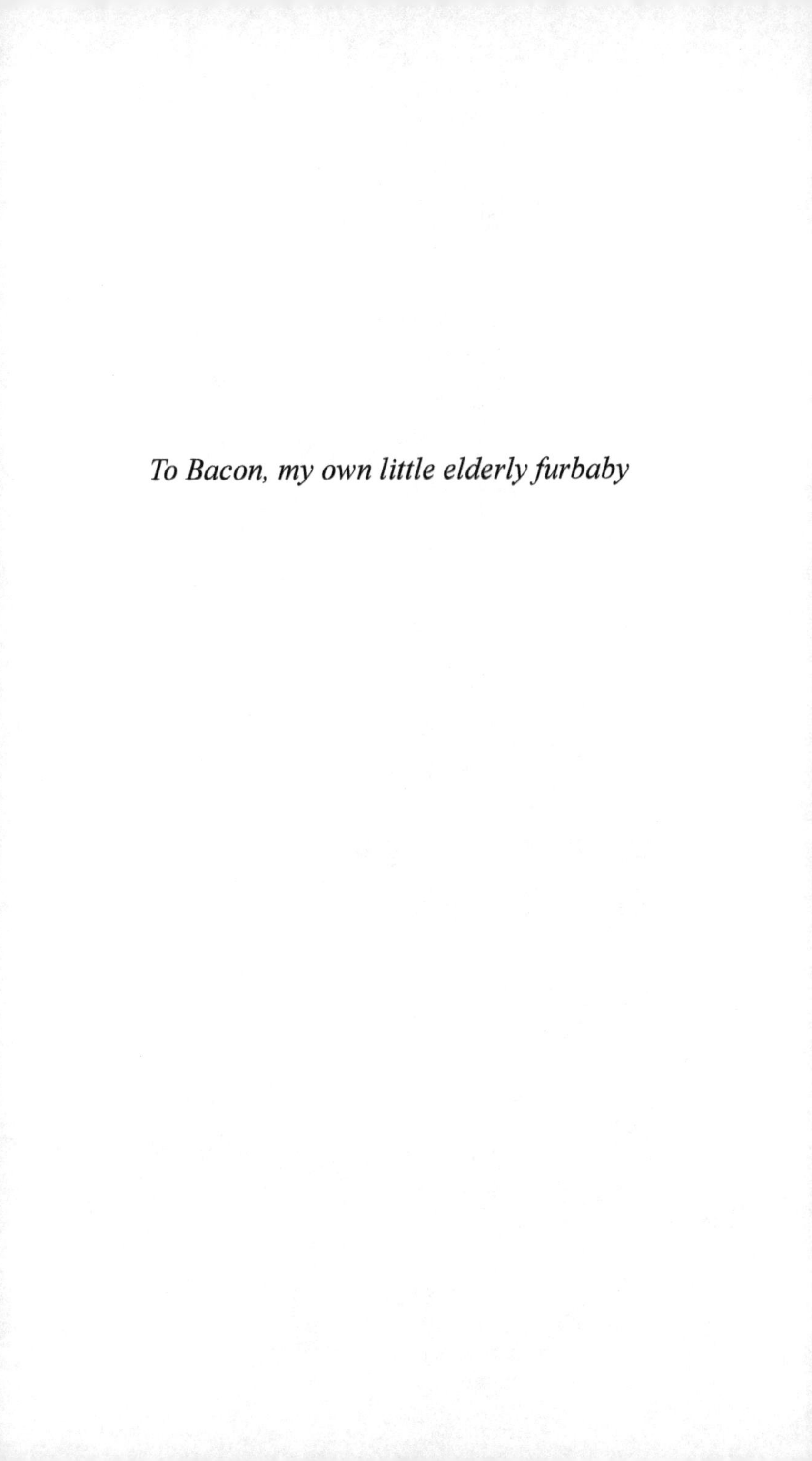

To Bacon, my own little elderly furbaby

CHAPTER 1
NICLAS

"Happy birthday to me." Niclas came up out of the middle of the River Wylve, eyeing the muddy coins in his hand. He shifted his waterproof metal detector under his other arm. "Well, aren't you pretty specimens?"

"Oi. Professor Dirt. Swim this way. I've brought cake." His brother whistled sharply from the riverbank. "C'mon, Nic, I'd wager you forgot lunch."

"I didn't." Niclas glowered at his older brother, Izan. "I had breakfast. Who are you wagering with? It's just you."

"Ready Brek dosed with more sugar than is healthy doesn't count as a meal." Izan grinned at him while Niclas grumbled under his breath. "Stop

cursing at me in ye olde English. You could just use 'fuck.' The world won't end if you do."

"I enjoy using old words. It's fun. 'Sard' basically means 'fuck' anyway." Niclas collected interesting curses almost as much as he did ancient artefacts. "Etymology is fascinating."

"And people think you're talking about sardines or something." Izan dodged the spray of water Niclas sent at him. "Are you coming or not? I can hear your stomach grumbling from over here."

"No, you can't."

The Ruiz brothers were polar opposites in many aspects despite being almost identical in looks. They were often teased for being twins born ten years apart. Both had dark brown eyes and hair. Izan kept his close-cut, while Niclas had a shaggy, longish mane of wavy curls.

The differences only expanded from there. Niclas was a twenty-eight-year-old autistic man. His hands were scarred from years of working on archaeological digs for the British Museum, though in all honesty, he blamed his own clumsiness for most of his healed injuries. His entire life revolved around archiving treasures and hunting for them in his spare time.

Izan had served in the military—and hadn't struggled with anything other than a drive to push himself harder and farther than anyone else around him. He stood both taller and a little broader than his younger brother. Protective by nature, he tended toward an organised and regimented life, not something Niclas found interesting or comfortable.

For Niclas, a lot of life had been a struggle. He'd worked harder to keep up when others found things easy. It was sometimes exhausting.

Things in general often came easily to Izan. On the other hand, Niclas stumbled his way into success and failure in equal measure, often with a bruise or two to show for his effort. Spatial awareness had always been an issue for him—thanks to being autistic—something his elder brother didn't struggle with at all.

Izan had dated his way through quite a few men and women over the years. Niclas had been hesitant to enter relationships. His asexuality tended to be a barrier for some.

The brothers adored one another. Izan had always looked out for him, which Niclas found both endearing and frustrating. He knew his brother meant well.

"Still planning your extended walk around the Cornish beaches over June and July? Have you thought about bringing a friend with you?" Izan offered him one of the small cakes he'd brought. "Eat, eat."

"I'll be fine." Niclas had endured this argument twice already. "I've planned everything out quite carefully."

"Fine? Fine. Fine, he says." Izan wiped the crumbs from his shirt with precise meticulousness. "Last trip, you almost drowned, and you broke two toes. The one before? You got lost for three days. Three days."

"I wasn't lost. Just… took longer than expected to locate where I'd parked my Mini Cooper." Niclas crossed his arms and glared at his brother. "I got there eventually."

"Three whole days?" Izan raised an eyebrow at him. "You found it when a team came to rescue you."

"I found a stash of coins. The oldest I've ever discovered," Niclas protested. "We're still cataloguing them at the museum. And they'll pay for this entire trip and probably the one after."

Izan pinched the bridge of his nose. He did that a lot around his younger brother. "Please be careful. I'm already starting to go grey."

"You're old," Niclas teased him. "Don't blame me for the passage of time taking its toll on you."

"Ancient rubbish isn't more valuable than your life."

"I don't intentionally get lost or injured." He had a bad habit of getting hyper-fixated on a new treasure hunt or arching project to the exclusion of just about everything else in his life. "I try to be careful. I promise to do my best not to get hurt."

"So where's this Airbnb? I've driven all this way. Why don't we pick up a pizza or something? You can tell me all about your finds." Izan glanced down at Niclas's wetsuit. "You leave your clothes in the Mini?"

"It's a little cottage on the outskirts of Warminster. The owner's connected to the museum. He gave me a good deal for the month." Niclas had varied successes with his treasure hunts. One a few years ago had garnered him a decent amount of money even after splitting it with the landowner. Izan had insisted he invest it wisely, and as a result, he could afford to travel across the country a few times a year. "I planned to be here for another couple of hours."

"The river, silt, and relics aren't going to vanish in a day. And you need more than a white chocolate and raspberry cupcake." Izan took the metal detector from his brother, allowing him to more easily carry the small waterproof bag he had brought to store his treasures in while swimming. "I parked beside your Mini Cooper, so we'll have to walk back."

"I really wanted to—"

"Niclas." Izan sighed. He shook his head before taking a deep breath. "It's your birthday. Maybe I just want to spend a little time with you."

"Fine." He wasn't trying to be difficult, but a change in his schedule always made him grumpy while he tried to process the new plan. "It's not far. I tried to stay close to my car this time."

"This time? What happened?"

"Nothing." Niclas didn't think his brother needed to know he'd had to hitch a ride with a local priest when he'd somehow managed to exhaust himself diving. "I just meant in general."

With another one of his long sighs, Izan started walking along the riverbank toward their vehicles. They'd been on their own for a while. Their father had passed away before Niclas was born; their mother had died of cancer when he was thirteen.

Their stepfather was a lovely Welshman with his head in his books, something Niclas had obviously learned from him. Izan had often taken care of both of them.

Their only other living relatives were grandparents who still lived in Spain. They hadn't seen them in years. So it meant the brothers were incredibly close.

And it meant occasionally, Izan acted more like his father.

"So, what did you find?" Izan broke the silence after a few minutes of walking. "Anything interesting?"

Niclas cheered up immediately. He shifted his gear under his other arm to bring up one of the tokens that he'd cleaned up. "Copper, I think. A bracelet that's definitely Roman. Not sure of the precise date, but I'm thinking around the third century. Maybe."

"Nice." Izan leaned over to get a closer look at it. "Rare?"

"Not exceptionally, but a nice artefact none-theless." He carefully secured it back in his little trea-sure pouch. "Shouldn't you be working? Playing the looming bodyguard behind some CEO?"

"Private security isn't all CEOs."

"No? Who else can afford your services?"

"Fair point." Izan shrugged. He glanced at Niclas for a moment with an odd look on his face. "I have a favour to ask."

"No."

"I haven't asked yet."

"You've got a weird gleam in your eyes. I love

you. I don't trust the look when I don't understand it." Niclas trusted his brother, but sometimes Izan did things that irritated him. "What is it?"

"Remember Falk?"

"Falk." Niclas cringed when his voice went up almost an octave. He cleared his throat and ignored his brother's chuckle. "The tall Viking? Who you call Grizz? Why are you acting like I've only met him once?"

"He's not a Viking."

"Falk Evensen? Taller than you? Blond hair and blue eyes? Definitely a Viking in a past life. Or, maybe part bear combined with a Nordic ancestor." Niclas ignored how his heart always started racing when he thought about his brother's old military mate and current co-worker. "He's one of your best mates. I've known him almost as long as you have. Of course I remember him. What about him?"

Falk Evensen had been a combat medic. He'd saved Izan's life once. There was something of a brave warrior in him, maybe his Viking ancestry shining through.

"He's planning on taking a few months off. Too much stress. I thought maybe you wouldn't mind a companion on your Cornwall adventure?" Izan threw

an arm out to catch him when Niclas tripped. "How…
how do you stumble over the sodding air?"

"Talent?"

"What do you think?"

What do I think?

*Invite the man that I've had a crush on for over
ten years to travel with me for the summer?*

What could possibly go wrong?

"Think about what? Tripping over the air?" Niclas
inspected his shoes for a second. "Maybe the ground
tried to eat my foot?"

"Not about tripping. About Falk joining you on
your trip?"

"I'm sure he can manage on his own without his
own personal disaster human stumbling around him."
Niclas didn't know if his heart and mind could take
two months of being close to Falk Evensen without
imploding or eventually humiliating himself.

"Listen, just promise me you're going to be
careful on this trip." Izan threw his arm around his
brother's shoulders. "You're fully capable of taking
care of yourself, but try not to drown or get lost or
accidentally trip off a cliff. And think about Falk."

I already think about him—far too much.

They were both asexual. It was a conversation that
had come up a few years prior while Falk was trying

to explain his sexuality to Izan. It led Niclas to do the same.

Gay was something Izan understood. Asexuality had been confusing. Niclas had appreciated Falk's help since he often stumbled over words, even when figuring things out for himself.

They'd commiserated over similar frustrations by explaining how they could be attracted to someone without it being sexual. Love someone without wanting to engage in more than kissing or touching. Intercourse had never interested Niclas—or Falk, from what he'd said.

And now I'm back to thinking about him again.

He's never shown any interest in dating me.

I don't need a broken heart.

CHAPTER 2
FALK

"You can see me through the glass door of my office. And we were in the same meeting an hour ago. So, yes, Izan, I am in." Falk narrowed his eyes at his friend. They'd served together in the military. He'd been a combat medic within the same unit as Izan, but he'd been medically discharged when post-traumatic stress had begun to take its toll on him. "What do you want?"

"Professor Dirt."

Ah, shite.

Professor Dirt was their term of endearment for Izan's adorable younger brother. The clumsy and brilliant Niclas. The most accident-prone human being on

the planet. And the person who'd stumbled his way right into Falk's impenetrable heart.

"What about Niclas?" Falk decided to get straight to the point of the conversation. He could play it cool. Definitely. No reason to seem nervous at all. The less he thought about the younger Ruiz, the better it would be for his heart. "Did he enjoy his birthday?"

"He did. He's going on this two-month treasure hunt around the beaches and rivers of Cornwall. Backpacking with his metal detectors." Izan frowned at the idea. While he was proud of his brother, Falk knew he worried. Constantly. "I had an idea."

"Oh, shite." Falk prepared himself for yet another "idea" from his best friend. "Go on, then. Let me bask in your brilliance."

"Wanker. Fine. Listen, what if I paid you to play bodyguard? Keep him from drowning himself in the sea or taking a header off a cliff. How many times in the past year have you said you needed a vacation? Take a couple of months and enjoy Cornwall. And keep my baby brother from breaking yet another body part." Izan was working hard to sell him on the idea. "Please?"

"You're not paying me to be your brother's keeper."

"Why not? This is a private security company."

Izan shrugged indifferently when Falk groaned. "How is this any different from our usual clients?"

"First, I'm your boss. It's my company. The client is also usually aware that they're being protected." Falk warred internally with himself. He'd enjoy spending time with Niclas, but this had disaster written all over it. "You're not paying me."

"Come on, Falky."

"No, I'm not being paid to watch out for Niclas. He'd be mortified if he found out and angry with both of us. Justifiably so." Falk stared down at his desk calendar. He'd cleared off the next two months since he'd desperately needed a break. "Here's what I'm going to do. First, I'll talk to your brother. I'll join him for at least a few weeks if he doesn't mind my hanging around."

"Thank you." Izan seemed genuinely relieved.

Falk smirked at him. "Don't thank me yet. You're going to be in charge while I'm gone. That means making sure all our ongoing contracts are handled."

"Oh, you—"

"Careful, I can still kick your arse." Falk dodged the packet of crisps Izan tossed at him. "Thanks for the snack."

A few weeks later, against his better judgement, Falk found himself driving to Cornwall. The over two-hour drive to Bude, where Niclas's first Airbnb was located, gave him plenty of time to second guess his decision. If nothing else, he was about to have a lovely two-month vacation.

From the moment they met, he'd liked Niclas more than he should. Izan had been his closest friend since they'd met in training. It made him hesitant to act on those feelings.

The blue cottage was a beautiful little place situated at the top of a cliff. Falk could see the coastal path running alongside it and a trail that obviously led down to the beach. He parked behind Niclas's Mini Cooper, seeing no other signs of the man.

Falk grabbed his bag and headed up to the cottage. He knocked on the door but got no answer, so he made his way around the back to peer through the windows. "Nic?"

Dropping his bag by the sliding doors at the rear of the cottage, Falk wandered down to the end of the wooden deck and peered down at the beach. He finally spotted Niclas a ways off—or a speck that he thought might be him.

It took Falk fifteen minutes to wind his way down the path leading to the beach. He enjoyed the warm May weather and the salty air off the sea. Unfortunately, the wind picked up halfway down.

The beach was surprisingly empty. Falk eyed the sea, wondering when high tide was. He hoped Niclas had paid attention to the times. It was definitely something that he'd forget to do.

"Nic." Falk immediately regretted surprising him when Niclas stood up from where he'd been inspecting something amidst the rock and sand, stumbling backwards and falling back. "*Shite*. You all right?"

"Been better." Niclas scrambled to his feet and brushed off his jeans. "Thought you were arriving around three or four in the afternoon."

"It's five."

"Ah." He shoved his metal detector under one arm and then pulled his phone out of his pocket. "So it is. Lost track of time." Niclas bent down to grab a plastic tub that he carefully stored in a mesh bag. He peered up at the cliff behind Falk. "I've been putting off the trek back up to the cottage."

"Here. Let me help."

"I can manage." Niclas caught his toe on a rock and fell into Falk's arms. "Or… not."

"Why don't I carry the metal detector for you?" Falk enjoyed the briefest moment of having Niclas in his arms, then helped steady him on his feet. "Did you have lunch?"

"I brought snacks."

Snacks with Niclas could mean anything from an Aero bar to a massive bowl of ramen. Falk decided not to push him on the subject. Instead, they'd grab dinner once they made it up to the cottage.

It was clear on the journey up the path that Niclas's energy had begun to fade. Falk wondered how long he'd been out on the beach. Where had he started?

They made it up to the top of the cliff. The journey took twice the time it had for him to make his way down to the beach. Niclas sat on the nearby wooden fence and caught his breath; he dug around in his bag to retrieve a water bottle.

After a minute or two, they continued to the pretty blue cottage in the distance. Niclas fished out his keys and opened the door while Falk retrieved his bag. He dropped it into the room that would be his and returned to the kitchen to inspect the contents of the fridge.

"I bought food," Niclas muttered defensively when he noticed Falk by the fridge. "Actual food. I can cook."

"I'm aware. You make the best ramen I've ever had." Falk found all the items required to make one of his favourite meals. "How about I whip up breakfast for dinner?"

Leaving him to it, Niclas darted away for a shower. Falk busied himself frying up sausage, bacon, and eggs. He also inspected the map stretched out on the little kitchen table.

There were multiple Xs all along the Cornish coastline, and a few rivers had also been highlighted. Niclas had a busy summer planned for himself. Falk hoped he could enjoy the adventure with him.

"Did Izan send you to keep me from drowning?" Niclas posed the blunt question once they'd settled down to dinner. "He claimed you needed rest."

"I do. And he did."

"Oh." Niclas became hyper-focused on his plate. "So…"

"I'm here because I desperately need a break." Falk decided to risk a little more honesty than was probably wise. "And spending time with you is never a hardship."

CHAPTER 3
NICLAS

Summertime in Cornwall was busy. Niclas rose early each morning to explore the beaches without crowds. He intended to travel around the entire coast from one side to the other and then head inland to treasure hunt through the rivers. It had taken him months and months to obtain all the necessary permissions and permits from authorities and landowners.

Fees had been paid. Niclas had reached out to the landowners along his planned route, where required, to make deals on handling the treasure he found. Most didn't mind since he was sticking to rivers and beaches; he wouldn't be digging up anyone's fields or gardens.

When Falk called to invite himself on the journey,

Niclas knew Izan had shoved his nose where it didn't belong. But still, he couldn't say no. He'd enjoy the company.

He'd enjoy *Falk's* company.

His plan for today was to move further south to another stretch of beach. Niclas had woken up at five in the morning. It gave him time to clean his gear and take a hot shower.

"Morning."

"Oh for…" Niclas placed a hand on his chest. "What are you doing in the dark?"

"Light's on." Falk gestured to the kitchen light behind him. "Not dark."

"What are you doing up?" Niclas hadn't drunk enough coffee to explain that Falk was actually standing in the shadows of the living room. "It's five in the morning."

"Heard your alarm. I thought I'd get coffee and breakfast going while you showered. I woke up at four." Falk followed Niclas into the kitchen. He already had a large travel mug in his hand. "Figured we'd go the easy route with bacon sarnies."

"I eat."

"Okay," Falk agreed easily.

Niclas narrowed his eyes at the man. "Okay. Maybe I forget sometimes, but it's not on purpose."

"Okay." Falk handed him a plate with a perfectly toasted bacon sandwich. "I had mine already."

"Why would you voluntarily wake up at four in the morning?"

"War leaves us with a lot of memories—and sleepless nights." Falk sipped his coffee slowly, leaning against the kitchen counter. "Some days, it's better to just get up and get on with my day instead of wallowing in the memories and pretending to rest."

Niclas had never considered the full ramifications of what his brother, Falk, and others like them had experienced during combat. He knew Izan had spent extensive time in therapy when he'd retired from the military. "I'm sorry."

"For?"

"I'm sorry you're in pain." Niclas set his plate on the counter. He awkwardly hugged Falk, who looped one of his arms around Niclas's back for the briefest moment before they separated. "I'm just going to go… eat my bacon sarnie. In there. Over there. I'm going to go."

Fleeing the kitchen with his plate and mug of coffee, Niclas inhaled his breakfast. Maybe if he went outside, the sea breeze would wash the blush from his face. He didn't often hug people, usually just his brother and grandparents when he saw them.

Mostly his brother.

The sun was just rising over the horizon when Niclas began lugging his gear out of the cottage. He had a bag with a large water bottle and snacks, along with other supplies. A container to safely store treasures. A backpack with a tablet for research and his camera, along with spare batteries for his metal detector.

Niclas left everything beside his Mini Cooper. He went to the side of the gravel road to peer out across the sea. The sky reminded him of sherbet with oranges and pinks. He heard the door open and shut. "Heading out?"

"Why don't I drive you? My vehicle's more comfortable." Falk bent down to pick up two of the bags and carry them to the back of his Range Rover Defender. "I planned to run on the beach this morning anyway. We can have lunch later."

"Don't malign my Mini."

"I have heated seats."

"Fine." Niclas went over to pick up his metal detector and placed it carefully beside the rest of his gear in the boot of the vehicle. "Why'd you really come out here? You could've vacationed anywhere. Following me around doesn't sound like a relaxing time. Izan always talks about wild parties and the like."

"I don't do wild parties." Falk waited for him to step back, then slammed the hatch shut. "Nic."

"Yes?"

Falk watched him for a second before seeming to change his mind. "Can you accept I might have found the idea of a vacation in Cornwall attractive?"

"I could." Niclas went to get into the vehicle and decided to let the conversation rest. He wasn't going to get a full answer. Maybe Falk didn't even know why. There were two months to suss it out. "But I wouldn't believe you."

In those first days, Niclas had managed to cover the first section of the beach on his list but hadn't found anything beyond a belt buckle, a toy soldier, and a few coins. Nothing the museum would want. Today he planned to move a bit further south. Falk drove them to the Viewing Point North car park along Marine Drive. It would allow them to walk down the coastal path to Widemouth Beach.

Consolidating some of the items into one back-pack, Niclas grabbed it and his metal detector. The rest could stay in the vehicle. He trekked down the path with Falk following close behind like a tall, looming shadow.

The north end of the beach was completely empty. Far too early for anyone else to be out. Niclas tried to keep what he carried on his back relatively light. He could spend hours scanning an area, and even the lightest weights could be painful after a while.

"I'm going to jog along the beach for a while. I'll come back in a bit, okay? We can grab lunch at the café together." Falk waited for Niclas to nod, then moved down the beach to begin doing stretches.

Oh for…

Why is he doing that there? Is he doing a split? Is that normal?

Oh my god.

He saw me staring at him.

Niclas turned on his metal detector and got to work. Ancient coins weren't obnoxiously tall and fit. They didn't have blue eyes that always seemed to catch him staring. Buried treasures had no impact on his blood pressure. *Don't look at him.*

"Nic."

He studiously kept his attention on the patch of sand where he'd been scanning. "Yeah?"

"It's safe to look. I'm done stretching."

"Saddle-goose."

"If you're going to go Shakespearean on me, I'll

just jog on." Falk winked when Niclas glanced over at him. "Please be careful."

"Not Shakespeare. Just means ridiculous."

"Me or you?" Falk jogged over to him.

"Both of us." Niclas moved to another section of the beach.

My heart's a fool.

Please be careful with it.

CHAPTER 4
FALK

"Oh, honestly, Ruiz, why are you even out here?"

The snide comment had been loud enough for Falk to hear it over the wind and waves. He'd been making his way slowly back down the beach. He'd stopped to watch Niclas from a distance.

Niclas was so fixated on scanning a small section of the beach, Falk wondered if he even realised the person was mocking him. She also had a metal detector and was dressed like she'd walked out of a movie about archaeologists.

But an insulting and dramatised version of archaeologists.

"Ruiz? Are you listening? How are you even affiliated with the museum at this point? It's dreadful."

"Nic." Falk strode forward, intent on moving whoever the person was along. "Everything all right?"

Nic acknowledged him with a shrug. His gaze was firmly focused on his metal detector. "Fine."

"Not going to introduce us?" She smiled at Falk.

He ignored her. "Nic? Why don't we take a break?"

"I'm Charlene. Charlene Ferguson." She held a manicured hand out towards him. Falk continued to ignore her, so she sidestepped Niclas to get closer. "I work closely with the British Museum on historical finds."

Falk shoved his hands into the pockets of the hoodie he'd worn. She made him think of a shark who wanted to get her teeth into him. "Fascinating. And that's different from Niclas, how?"

"I…" She reared back as if he'd struck her. "Ruiz—"

"Why don't you move along? I'm sure the lighting is better down the beach." Falk had no intention of indulging whatever issue she had with Niclas. He moved around her, dismissing her completely. "You ready for a break? Maybe walk down to the café for a bite and a cup of tea?"

"Sure."

With a huff of irritation, Charlene swanned off in a cloud of perfume. Falk fought not to chuckle. He'd half expected her to stamp her foot.

"You don't have to allow her to dismiss you like that." Falk knew Niclas hated confrontation. But Charlene Ferguson had been passive-aggressively vile throughout the conversation. "Is she always like that with you?"

"She doesn't mean anything by it." Niclas shrugged. "None of them do."

"She does." Falk knew from what Izan had told him how Niclas often missed certain social cues. "Who's them?"

"Oh." Niclas toyed with his metal detector. Finally, he pulled off his headphones and rested them around his neck. "I can't always tell."

"You haven't answered my question."

"What question?" Niclas crouched down to stow his headphones safely away. He grabbed his metal detector and backpack. "Café's just down the beach."

"You said 'none of them do.'"

"Just a few of Charlene's toadies. They're harmless. The director at the museum chases them off if they're being too obnoxious. Everyone else is lovely." Niclas shrugged. He didn't seem to understand why Falk was so bothered. "I'm quite focused when I'm cataloguing treasures. Focused and efficient. Faster than everyone else. Izan always told me to ignore people who can't appreciate my abilities."

"He's not wrong." Falk glanced back in the direction where Charlene had gone. "How'd she find you?"

"Museum insists on us sharing our treasure hunting itineraries. It's ostensibly to prevent us from doubling up in the same location at the same time." Niclas nodded his head toward where they could still see Charlene. "As you can see, some people use it for other purposes."

Giving another shrug, Niclas moved further down the beach. The Widemouth Bay Café had a line of people queuing. Falk heard him sigh loudly, then pushed forward to join at the back.

"Why don't you find a place for us to sit, and I'll order?" Falk could see Niclas almost vibrating with anxiety at the level of noise from the other beachgoers. "What do you want?"

Ultimately, Falk ordered two pork and apple burgers with a side of dirty fries. The latter was a delicious combination of chips topped with pulled pork, melted cheese, and BBQ sauce. He got them two cups of tea and a couple of little cakes to complete their meal.

Juggling his lunch bounty, Falk searched for Niclas. He finally spotted him on a spot of grass above the beach. It took a few minutes to get to him.

"Peaceful up here. Less screaming children." Niclas had clearly been going through his morning's finds and taking photos of them. "I don't usually break for lunch."

"I'm aware." Falk had heard Izan whinge endlessly about his younger brother, who tended to lose himself in hunting for historical treasures. He handed one of the burgers and mugs over, then set the platter of chips between them. "Figured we could share."

It was one of the best burgers Falk had eaten. The chips went quickly. They were an amazing combination of flavours.

When they finished, Niclas stretched back on the grass and stared up at the sky. He closed his eyes. Falk wondered what he was thinking while they watched the clouds pass.

"I found a button." Niclas sat up and opened the box where he stored his finds. He held up a brownish-grey domed object, flipping it over to show the attachment loop on the back. "Think it's probably a lead alloy. Maybe sixteenth century."

"Do you ever wonder how things wound up where you find them?"

Niclas became wholly focused on the button. He'd turned shy, which he'd never been around Falk. "Sometimes."

"Nic? Talk to me, Professor Dirt."

"I make up stories in my head about the owners." Niclas rubbed along the tiniest of cracks on the button, one that Falk would've missed if the sun hadn't been shining just so. "See this? Something damaged it. Maybe that's why it fell off."

"An arrow strike?" Falk kept his face serious. He didn't want Niclas to think he was poking fun at him. "Maybe a highwayman."

"A lovers' tryst that led to a duel?" Niclas put it away and returned the box to his bag. "Ready to walk back? I planned to check out Millook Haven before I wrapped up for the day."

"For metal detecting?"

"Maybe. A bit rocky for it, but mostly it's a lovely place to watch the sunset." Niclas gathered up their rubbish from lunch. "It's not far from here, though we should drive."

After getting rid of their rubbish, they made their way down the beach towards the car park. Falk found himself enjoying the silence with Niclas. He'd noticed the younger man preferred not to fill every pause with awkward small talk.

And small talk, in Falk's vast experience from running his business, was always awkward. He didn't consider himself either introverted or shy. Then again, maybe his combat service had provided enough chaotic noise and chatter to last a lifetime.

They found the little trail leading off the beach up the cliff to the coastal path. It was narrow and rocky. Falk kept a careful eye on Niclas, who had a tendency toward tripping at the best of times.

Falk took a step, the toe of his trainer caught on a stone, and down he went. He landed on his hands and knees with a painful thud. "Fuck."

The irony was not lost on him. Izan had sent him to keep Niclas from having accidents, and he was the one on his knees. He sat back on his heels to assess the damage.

Niclas retraced his steps and crouched in front of Falk, who grinned sheepishly. "Is being clumsy contagious? I'm usually the one with bruised knees and scraped-up hands."

Before Falk could respond, Niclas had dug through his backpack for a water bottle and a first aid kit. He poured water over Falk's hands to rinse them off. His fingers gently checked for any scrapes or wounds.

Falk tried not to react to those fingers caressing his hands. "Am I going to live, Dr Dirt?"

"A close thing, but yes. Shouldn't that be 'professor'?"

"Not when you're offering first aid. Want to kiss them better?" Falk expected him to pull away laughing. But, instead, Niclas's nimble fingers slipped down to his wrist. He lifted his hand up and grazed his lips against his palm. "A miracle cure."

Niclas's breath tickled Falk's skin for a second before he dropped his hand. "All better."

CHAPTER 5
NICLAS

THE LANES LEADING TO MILLOOK HAVEN WERE something out of an ancient forest. The road cut through the hill with wild trees that came alive in the wind. It was a stark contrast to being down on the beach with the water, sun, and sand.

Niclas half expected to see an Ent stepping into the road in front of them. He gestured to the gnarled branches that seemed to wind their way above the hedgerows. They danced almost macabrely in the wind. "I always feel as though I've stepped through the looking glass into a forgotten land out here."

Millook Haven was one of the quieter beaches in the area. Niclas visited whenever he came to Cornwall for a treasure hunt. It held special memories for him.

"Think your brother mentioned this place to me once," Falk commented after pulling into one of the few parking spots near the entrance to the little cove. "The name stood out."

"Izan brought me here when I was ten or eleven. He had a week's break from training." Niclas smiled at the memory. "He'd asked what I wanted for my birthday—and all I could think about was going to the beach. But I panicked at the crowds. He found Millook Haven and a couple of other out-of-the-way places."

"Sounds like Izan."

Niclas nodded. His brother always tended to go out of his way for people he cared about. "I remember the first time we came; I took a stone from the beach. I never knew you weren't supposed to, and I panicked. So I made him drive us back out here in the middle of the night so I could put the pebble back."

Falk gave a hearty, booming laugh. Niclas forced a grin; he didn't want to show how the sound had seemed to reverberate through his body in pleasant ways. "I can just imagine you panicking."

"Yes, well." Niclas picked up the pace a little. He carefully made his way down the beach, paying attention to not trip on the rocks. They'd already had one slip-up. "I found my first treasure here."

"Oh?"

"Well, I was ten. I thought it was a treasure." Niclas smiled fondly at the memory. "Izan didn't understand my excitement at finding a broken toy soldier. I still have it on a shelf in my flat."

Falk easily kept up with him. They were heading to the right of the beach when Niclas smashed his toe into one of the larger rocks. He stumbled forward, only to be caught and dragged back up to his feet. "Easy there, Professor Dirt."

"Sorry." Niclas had swung around with the momentum from Falk's pull. They were suddenly chest to chest. "I…"

Falk bent his head down towards him. "Are you all right?"

Why was he moving closer? Their lips were so close. So close. He could almost taste the kiss.

Niclas couldn't breathe. It was going to happen. A kiss. Maybe a start of something with someone he'd admired from afar. *Don't get carried away. You're getting carried away.* Their lips were a whisper apart when his phone rang. Izan's tone. *Sard.* He jerked away from Falk, dug in his pocket for his mobile, and answered the call. "Hello? Shouldn't you be working?"

"You okay? You sound weird."

"I'm fine."

"*Right.*"

"I am," Niclas insisted.

"Right." Izan was quiet for a second. "*Right.* How goes the hunt? Discovered King Arthur's knob yet? I mean sword."

"You're not funny."

"I'm hilarious." Izan laughed loudly as though to prove his point. "Have you seen Grizz much?"

"You sent him to be my bodyguard. What do you think?" Niclas began meandering along the beach with his back to Falk. He hoped the cool breeze would deal with the sudden flush on his neck and face. "Wasn't he enough? Do you also have to call to ensure I've tumbled into the sea?"

"Nic."

"For your information, the only person who's almost had a bad fall is Falk," Niclas grumbled. He didn't think it was entirely fair to treat him like he was fragile. "I don't always have accidents."

"How many times have you stubbed a toe or bumped into something on this trip?"

"I…." Niclas briefly considered chucking his phone into the sea. He didn't want the hassle of getting a new one, though. "Once. Okay, maybe three times. Four at the absolute most."

Izan sighed heavily. He was silent for a few moments before continuing. "You having fun? Remembering to eat at least a few times a day?"

"Yes, Mum, I'm having fun at camp. I'll write soon." Niclas grinned when Izan burst out laughing. "My trip has barely started. Ask me again when I'm a few weeks into it and regretting all my life choices."

"All of them?"

Niclas risked a glance back at Falk, who was wandering in the opposite direction to allow him some privacy. "Maybe not all of them."

The two brothers caught up for several minutes. Niclas finally managed to wind the conversation down. He wasn't overly fond of talking on the phone but made an exception for Izan.

There had been times over the years when his brother was serving in the military that they hadn't been able to talk often. He'd worried about Izan. Dreaded receiving a visit to tell him the worst had happened. So, he tried never to take him for granted.

The sun wasn't quite so high in the sky. Niclas was tired and ready to call it a day; it had been a slightly chaotic one for him. He whistled for Falk, who'd wandered far away from him.

He wanted the day to end. To get a little space from Falk and process the apparent changes happening in their relationship. It was pointless to even try to do any more detecting.

Falk jogged over to him. "Ready?"

"Yes." Niclas couldn't think of a single thing to say to the man.

It was awkward. All Niclas could think about was the almost kiss and Izan's interrupting it. He mumbled one-word answers to anything Falk said on the journey back to the vehicle.

The drive was no less painful. Words kept getting stuck in his throat. He wanted their easy camaraderie back.

And maybe a kiss.

"Do you want to—" Falk tried for the umpteenth time to draw him into a conversation while they exited the Range Rover.

"Have supper and an early night?" Niclas scrambled to grab his gear from the back of the vehicle. "Good idea."

Ignoring Falk's attempt to help, Niclas struggled toward the cottage with all his gear. Izan's call had left him flustered and embarrassed. He still wanted the ground to swallow him up whole.

It hadn't been how Niclas hoped a first kiss might go with Falk. Not interrupted by his wildly overprotective brother, who'd known something was off.

And it had all been going so well.

Until it wasn't.

Story of my life.

Don't get the song stuck in your head, don't get the song stuck in your head, don't get the song stuck in your head.

You don't even like the band.

Story of my life.

Sard.

Niclas dashed down the hall into the room and shut the door behind him. "Is this how my summer will go? Humiliation and awkwardness with a dash of crushed cans?"

CHAPTER 6
FALK

Izan had always been one of Falk's oldest and closest friends. Their bond had been forged through some of the best and worst moments of their lives, particularly in combat. As a result, he trusted him more than just about anyone else in the world.

The Ruiz brothers were two of the small number of people that Falk genuinely enjoyed being around. Unfortunately, he'd had the reputation in the service of being a grumpy bear. His nickname had been Grizzly for a number of reasons, including his height.

And he'd never wanted to dropkick his best mate into the ocean more than he currently did. It had almost been the perfect kiss. On a Cornish beach in the middle of summer.

An almost kiss.

Now Niclas had retreated into his shell like a spooked tortoise. Falk had followed him into the cottage, hoping to talk through the sudden awkwardness Izan had inserted into the situation. But instead, the younger man disappeared into his room.

Falk was standing in the kitchen, considering his options when his phone rang. He chuckled at the name on the screen. "Izan."

"Is he okay?"

"You spoke to him not thirty minutes ago."

"He sounded odd." Izan was incredibly rational about most things except his care and concern for his brother. "Off. He's never thrilled to be on the phone, but he practically hung up mid-conversation."

"Professor Dirt is perfectly fine. He had a long day. Probably just tired." Falk poked around the kitchen to find something for supper. "What do you know about Charlene Ferguson?"

Izan muttered a few choice words under his breath that Falk couldn't quite understand. "Is she still bothering Nic? I told him to report her. She's a wealthy woman with connected parents and an entourage who think she's going to take them places. But that doesn't make her untouchable. He deserves a calm work environment."

"Ah. One of those." Falk made a mental note to

keep an eye out for Charlene and her toadies. "He held his own."

"So he ignored her?" Izan seemed to know exactly what had happened.

"Basically." Falk pulled out the ingredients to whip up sandwiches with the leftovers in the fridge. "Anything else?"

"You're hurting my feelings. Both you and my brother wanting to rush me off the phone. Something going on down there?" Izan was teasing, but Falk heard a hint of suspicion in his voice.

"The only thing going on here is sun, sand, and a few coins and buttons." Falk pulled the slices of bread out of the bag. There was just enough to make something for both of them. "How're things going in the office?"

"Fine, fine. Keep your odd secrets. And keep my brother safe as well. Chat later." Izan disconnected the call before Falk had a chance to say anything else.

"Goodbye to you too." Falk set his phone down and scrubbed his fingers across his face with a groan. *Why do I just know this will all end in disaster?*

Footsteps drew him out of his thoughts. Falk focused on making sandwiches while waiting for Niclas to join him. He hoped the time alone had given him space to feel less awkward.

"Izan called you." Niclas came into the kitchen with a Rubik's Cube in hand. He twisted and turned it while staring over Falk's shoulder. "Why did he start calling you Grizz?"

"It happened in the military. Owing to my being rather growly in the morning and my overall size, I quickly earned the nickname Grizzly. One of our trainers was American. The name stuck." Falk sliced the sandwiches into halves.

"You're never growly with me."

"No. No, I'm not." Falk finally finished with the sandwiches and turned to face him.

"We almost kissed."

Falk drew on all his training to avoid grinning at Niclas's pure lack of artifice. "We did."

"Was it an accident?"

"Did I accidentally almost kiss you?" Falk didn't chuckle. He moved across the kitchen until he stood in front of Niclas. "I might stumble over rocks, and you may stub your toes, but our lips touching? Planned, intended, and enjoyed."

Niclas continued messing with his cube. He flipped it over and over in his hands, not really making any progress. "So, not an accident?"

"No."

"Definitely not an accident," he repeated.

"Definitely." Falk couldn't contain his grin. Niclas peeked up at him through the fringe of his brown hair.

"Sure?"

"We could repeat the conversation a few times if it would help." Falk closed the distance between them. He brought a hand up to cover Niclas's fidgeting fingers. "Or, we can put an end to the confusion?"

"Can we?"

"Now you're just messing with me by repeating things." Falk enjoyed the way Niclas's lips twitched into a smirk. He didn't want the day to end with almost kisses and second thoughts. He brought his hands up to frame Niclas's face. His thumb traced his stubble-covered jaw. "How about we cross the *t*'s and dot the *i*'s, so there are no doubts about whether we were going to kiss?"

"How do you cross the *t*'s on a kiss?"

Falk used his index finger to slowly draw a *T* over Niclas's lips. "Like that."

"Fal—"

Falk cut him off with a kiss. He tilted his head so their mouths lined up perfectly. His tongue flicked out to run along Niclas's bottom lip. "There… Nothing accidental about that."

"No, no, definitely not accidental." Niclas stumbled back, looking a little dazed. He held tightly to his Rubik's Cube. "I should… I'm just going to go. I'll go. Right. Going."

Falk tried not to chuckle when Niclas practically vanished in front of them. *That went well.*

Too much?

They'd spoken frequently about being asexual. Niclas had mentioned enjoying kissing but not much more. Falk felt the same.

Maybe they'd have to talk about it again.

CHAPTER 7

NICLAS

THE FOLLOWING MORNING, NICLAS DIDN'T HAVE TIME to think about kissing Falk or how his brother might react to it. He had a fairly tight schedule to keep on this particular trip. Between the Airbnb rentals and licenses required, he'd had to coordinate everything carefully to avoid missing out.

But it had been overwhelming in the best way possible.

The kiss.

Niclas lay in bed, staring out the window that offered a view across the cliff to the sea below. The sky had streaks of light beginning to show. He'd planned to be up early so he could pack up his things and do a quick whiz around the cottage before leaving.

He hadn't planned to be awake two hours before his alarm went off with his mind buzzing over a kiss.

Just a kiss.

Just a kiss.

Thirty minutes before his alarm, Niclas managed to force himself out of bed and reached out to turn it off. He rushed around, getting dressed and carrying his already packed bags to the front door. And he definitely didn't think more about how Falk's lips had felt against his.

"Here." Falk waved a plate in front of his face twenty minutes later. Niclas jerked back from where he'd been inspecting his gear for a second time. "Have breakfast. I know you've forgotten. Made you a coffee as well."

"I would've remembered." Niclas eyed the sandwich hungrily before admitting the truth. "Eventually. You're not tired of sandwiches, are you? I know Izan often worries about my obsession with bread-filled food."

"Sure." Falk sipped his own coffee. "I'm good with whatever makes you happy."

"I would've," Niclas mumbled around a mouthful of bacon and bread. He chased it down with a swig of perfectly made coffee. "Did I wake you?"

"Been up. Went for a jog and grabbed breakfast at

the neat little place up from the beach." Falk didn't seem nearly as grumpy as Izan always claimed him to be in the morning. At least, he didn't appear that way with Niclas. "You in a hurry?"

"Eager to move on to the next cottage and set of beaches." Niclas slowed down his eating ever so slightly. "Izan claims I get hyper-fixated when I'm on one of these trips."

"Do you?"

"I've never been interested in trains or numbers or any of those other things people assume autistics drown themselves in. Not my brand of quirk." Niclas finished up the last of his sandwich while peering around the room. "You following me to the cottage?"

"Of course." Falk took the plate from him. "About last night."

"Grizz."

"No, I just want to make sure kissing is okay." Falk was suddenly quite serious. He leaned across the table to take Niclas's hand. "I didn't make you uncomfortable?"

"No, no. I enjoyed it." Niclas managed to get the words out and hoped his face hadn't turned bright red from blushing. "I… enjoyed it, Grizz. I didn't want more."

"Me either. But the kissing…"

"Was brilliant?" Niclas finished for him.

Their next stop was a cottage outside of Port Isaac. There were multiple sites to the east and west he intended to visit. It was a cosy converted barn with views across the countryside down to the sea.

He wanted a find. Maybe two. But one good treasure would make the entire trip worth it.

"Are you genuinely going to follow me from cottage to cottage and beach to beach?" Niclas packed the last of his bags into the boot of his little vehicle. "Doesn't seem like the best sort of holiday."

"No clients? No gossiping employees? Just mostly sunny skies, crashing waves, and you for company." Falk had his large hands wrapped around the travel mug that he'd carried outside with him. It seemed tiny in comparison to his fingers. "Something wrong?"

Niclas jerked his gaze away from Falk's hands. He glanced back at the cottage. "I've got to leave the keys in the little drop box by the front door."

"You sure everything's okay?"

"Fine." Niclas jogged back to secure the keys before hopping into the relative safety of his car. *How do I not embarrass myself?*

A question Niclas had asked himself multiple times over the years. He'd usually ask Izan for advice.

His brother was brilliant at helping him navigate non-autistic conversational minefields.

This was definitely not one of the times he could call his brother. Izan tended to be overprotective at the best of times. Part of him was terrified that this would be an unmitigated disaster.

Everything felt different—mostly in a good way. Niclas didn't know how to act. Falk had been his usual self.

The drive to Port Isaac allowed far too much time to obsess over every nuance of their conversation, to the point that he didn't know if he could look Falk in the face. He forced himself to stop thinking about it.

Once they'd dropped off their bags at the new cottage, Niclas was ready to head to Bossiney Cove as his first stop. One of the smaller beaches, it wouldn't take him long to finish it.

There'd been good finds in and around Tintagel. Niclas hadn't been lucky himself, but he still enjoyed exploring the beach. The cliffs that towered on both sides and the rocky dip between them. It all made for fertile ground to hunt and for his imagination.

"Wasting more time, I see."

Niclas sighed. He heard the shrill tone of Charlene even with his headphones firmly on his head. He shifted them back and then glanced in her direction. "Did you want something?"

"Yes: you out of my way."

Out of her way?

What the devil is she talking about?

They'd been at odds from the moment Charlene had shown up at the museum and assumed she owned everything. Or, everyone seemed to think they were. Niclas mostly ignored her and her friends.

They seemed more like archaeologist cosplayers than people who were genuinely interested in doing the work. It was partly why she never showed up to archive any of the finds. Plebeian tasks weren't meant for her.

In her own words.

"Why are you here? You haven't gotten a license for this area. Not for the next week or so." Niclas continued scanning the sand, following his grid carefully to avoid missing a section. His nose twitched at the overpowering floral perfume that managed to blanket the salty sea air and made him want to sneeze. "Leave me alone."

"Oh. Does the silent boy have fangs?"

Niclas lifted his head to stare at Charlene's chin. His gaze narrowed on something the way it always did when he was stressed, hyper-focusing on something random to avoid becoming overwhelmed. "You have a long hair. Just there."

"Why, you…" She stormed off, leaving him to stare after her, completely baffled.

"What did I say?"

"Maybe don't mention stray hairs." Falk handed him a bottle of water. "It's warming up. You should hydrate."

"Why, if she didn't know there was a hair?"

"Trust me. Never mention hairs on someone's face. People can be… sensitive." Falk nudged the bottle in Niclas's hand. "Hydrate."

"People can be sensitive about hair?" Niclas decided to focus on drinking because the water was far less confusing than the rest of their discussion. "Don't explain it. I'm not sure I'll understand even if you try—and I'll only get more frustrated in the process."

"Just… keep hydrating, and trust me when I say you shouldn't mention chin hairs."

"Just chin hairs?" Niclas asked. He could hear Falk smothering a laugh.

"Not just chin hairs."

"This might actually be the most absurd conversation I've had." Niclas cracked a smile at Falk. "Ever."

CHAPTER 8

FALK

"How are things at the office?" Falk sat on a large boulder further down the beach from where Niclas was currently scanning with his metal detector. He'd gotten a call from Jess, one of his unit leaders. "Any fires to put out?"

"No fires aside from Izan trying to figure out if something's going on down there." Jess went quiet for a moment. He heard a door opening and then closing. "How goes Operation: Court the Nerd?"

"Jess."

"Yes?" She sounded the picture of innocence. "You know, boss, there's a new metal detector on the market. Might make a nice courting present for your intended."

"You've been watching *Bridgerton* again, haven't

you?" Falk kept an eye on Niclas in the distance. "Text me a link."

"Already pre-ordered one for you."

"That is *not* why you have access to my credit card." Falk sighed when she cackled gleefully on the other end of the line.

"What? No, thank you?" Jess was always irrepressible. She'd never even remotely deferred to him as a boss. It was one of the reasons she helped manage things in his absence. "I've also sent you a list of highly rated small restaurants. I'm sure Professor Dirt prefers quiet and cosy."

"Shit."

"Boss?"

"He just fell off a boulder into the sea. Don't tell Izan." Falk took off at a run, managing to shove his phone into his pocket. He plucked Niclas from where he was fighting with his metal detector. "Are you hurt?"

"Fine."

Falk got Niclas on relatively, given their location, solid ground. "Are you hurt? Did you break anything?"

Niclas ignored the question, opting to mutter a string of Shakespearean-sounding curses. "I'm fine."

"You're limping. Have a seat. Let me check your

ankle." Falk got him to sit on one of the large rocks nearby. He knelt down and began gently checking for injuries. "Don't think you've broken anything."

"Don't tell Izan," Niclas muttered.

"There's no need to be embarrassed." Falk tilted his head to peek at Niclas's flushed face. He had water dripping from his hair and clothes; even given the relative warmth of the day, the sea wouldn't have been a balmy temperature. "Did you happen to bring a change of clothes?"

"You aren't the one tumbling into the sea. Again. Not even my first or second time." Niclas gingerly rolled his ankle around. "Am I going to live, Dr Evensen?"

"Combat medic. Not an MD. And technically, I'm not officially anything since I've been discharged from the service." Falk sat back on his heels and released his hold on Niclas. "Think you're going to be fine, but we should head back to the cottage to get you dried off."

"I'll be fine."

"You'll be uncomfortable in damp clothing." Falk knew Niclas could be incredibly sensitive to clothing and other textures against his skin. He remembered Izan talking about struggling to get his younger brother to wear anything outside of a specific brand of

T-shirt as a pre-teen. "I imagine it'll be clammy and heavy after a dip in the salty sea."

"Fine, fine." Niclas was back to embarrassed and grumbly. He bent down to lift up his metal detector. "I'll have to check this as well. I didn't bring my submersible one today. Here's hoping I haven't wrecked it. Not exactly fully waterproof."

"Come on. You've had quite the morning. We can pick up something to eat to take back with us to the cottage." Falk stood up and helped Niclas up to his feet as well. "Fairly certain you haven't sprained it either. But… let's not go tripping over anything else if you can help it."

"Not like I've done it on purpose." Niclas closed his eyes for a second. He turned his face towards the breeze off the sea and inhaled deeply for a few moments. He finally glanced back over at Falk with a sheepish grin. "Sorry. I can't seem to be trusted on my own two feet."

"Everyone trips up, Nic. You're not alone."

"Fairly confident most people don't trip over their own feet at least once a day or bash themselves into the sides of door frames and furniture on a regular basis." Niclas gathered up his equipment. He hadn't found much of anything yet. "Isn't it too early for lunch?"

"Not by the time we've gotten away from the beach, packed up, found a place to pick up food, and driven to the cottage." Falk picked up one of the bags and the damp metal detector. "Come on. I've an idea of where we can grab something to eat."

True to her word, Jess had already sent him a selection of restaurants to visit. Nosebag was one not far from the cove. It had an interesting takeaway menu that he thought Niclas would appreciate.

They got a selection of tacos, quesadillas, and enough chips to feed an army. Maybe not the entire army. But they'd definitely gotten more than was probably necessary.

The drive back to the cottage from Tintagel was punctuated by the occasional grunts and groans from the passenger's seat. Niclas shifted repeatedly. Falk glanced over to find him holding his shirt away from his body.

Niclas muttered under his breath before yanking his shirt over his head, leaving him bare-chested. "Feels like moist sandpaper all over my skin. I hate it."

"Right." Falk forced his gaze away from the tawny flesh now exposed to him. Niclas spent much of his time outdoors, carrying things around. He swam a lot. He wasn't all sculpted muscle but more functionally fit. Lithe. Perfect, to his mind. "*Right.*"

"Why'd your voice go funny? Something wrong?"

Falk waved off Niclas's confused concern. "Fine. Everything is perfectly fine."

I haven't been staring at your upper body like I want to eat my lunch off it.

"Okay." Niclas sounded even more confused, but he let it go. "I've gotten water and sand all over your vehicle."

"I'll hoover it later. Nothing to worry about." Falk waved off his concern. "Trust me. It's seen worse."

"Really?"

"Your brother once dumped an entire container of curry on the backseat." Falk was relieved when Niclas finally relaxed enough to laugh with him. "We'd gotten a late supper for everyone at the office. He tripped and chucked the lot into the vehicle. It smelled like garlic and other spices for weeks."

"It could be worse."

"Yeah?"

"Could've been durian." Niclas sent a wicked smile in his direction.

"Would you mind terribly if I killed your brother?" Falk sighed. They'd once challenged themselves to eat durian, which, while a delicacy to some, smelt like the worst thing he'd ever had the misfortune to come across. He'd barely managed a minute before promptly spewing it back out. "He was sworn to secrecy."

"Jess told me."

"Ah. Of course, she did. Double agent Jess." Falk made a note to find a way to pay her back in kind. "After you've changed and we've had lunch, are you planning to head back out?"

"Possibly. I've a tight schedule to keep." Niclas held his damp T-shirt gingerly in his hands. "Somewhere closer by, perhaps. With fewer boulders."

"Maybe don't climb on them this time?"

"Helpful. Very, very helpful."

CHAPTER 9

NICLAS

Halloumi chilli fries were the perfect balm for a frustrating morning. Falk didn't seem to mind that he'd absconded with them. He had been entirely distracted by Niclas not wearing his shirt.

Maybe he hadn't even noticed.

Niclas had a quick but scalding shower. He changed into less crusty clothing and felt slightly better about the entire thing. His phone rang before he could leave his room. "Izan? Shouldn't you be working?"

"Shouldn't you be on a windy beach?"

"We came back to the cottage for lunch." Niclas tried to dance around the reason why. "We're going out again after. Why?"

"What happened?"

"Nothing."

"'Nothing' hasn't worked ever. You always say it with an odd lilt to your voice when something's happened." Izan called him out immediately.

"I fell into the sea. Again." Niclas slumped onto the bed with a groan. He fell back when Izan snickered on the other end of the phone. "Not injured. Falk plucked me out of the water. So nothing to worry about aside from my wounded pride."

"Falk won't poke fun."

"No, he wouldn't." Niclas couldn't stop the smile from spreading across his face when he thought about Falk picking him up. "He's a friendly grizzly."

"Falk? A friendly grizzly." Izan was quiet for a moment. "What's going—"

"Oh, must go. Lunch is getting cold. Love you." Niclas disconnected the call before his brother could finish his question. "Sard."

Putting his phone on silent, Niclas stared up at the overhead wooden beam. They'd done an amazing job in converting it. The whitewashed walls provided a beautiful contrast to exposed beams and charcoal-grey tiled floors.

It was a lovely little two-bedroom cottage. They'd managed to preserve the charm of the old barn while creating a comfortable living space. Niclas loved how the windows offered spectacular views across the countryside and out to the sea in the distance.

If Niclas had to pick one place in the world to live, he'd be hard-pressed to choose a more beautiful place. He pushed himself off the bed and went to peer outside. The sun was still out, glinting overhead; the best sort of day to be out on the beach.

Okay.

Walk out into the living room and have lunch. Nothing to be stressed about. It's not really a date.

Just... two people having a meal together after we've kissed.

Not technically a date, but not exactly not one either?

What the devil am I even saying?

"I really have to stop talking to myself." Niclas dragged his fingers roughly through his damp hair. He checked his shirt and jeans, but nothing was out of place. "Well? What am I waiting for? Divine intervention?"

There were a few more minutes of dithering before Niclas finally found the courage to leave the room. He reminded himself Falk had never poked fun at him. They could laugh together, but he'd never be cruel.

Ever.

"There you are. I was beginning to worry that you'd swanned off with the chips and drowned your sorrows in a shower." Falk was sitting at the little round dining table by the open window. "Saved you half of the tacos. The duck ones are particularly good."

"Izan called."

"Yeah?" Falk took a bite out of his last taco; juice dripped down his fingers. He brought his thumb up to lick it clean. "You okay?"

Niclas spun around and tried to take a deep breath without seeming like he was. It came out like a strangled cough instead. "Fine."

"Nic?"

"I'm fine." His voice cracked while he cursed himself for his inability to remain calm under pressure. "Fine."

One day, Niclas thought he might be able to seem cool, calm, and collected. And any other word that meant he didn't come across like a total fool. Today, however, was not going to be it.

"Something wrong?" Falk had moved closer while Niclas had been mentally spiralling over his tongue. His hands rested on Niclas's shoulders, pausing when he shook his head in response to the question. "Are you sure?"

"Confident."

The word came out without stuttering, a win in his mind. Niclas had expected a few things when Izan had fobbed his safety off on Falk. None of it had involved some of his most private fantasies coming true.

Or, maybe not coming true, but the vaguest hint they might.

He'd never once thought Falk might be interested in him. In his best friend's younger brother. In the stumbling, often bumbling archaeologist who played in the dirt. "I should eat my tacos."

"Go on then. I've a few phone calls of my own to make. Once you sort out your metal detector, we can head back out if you want." Falk's fingers danced across Niclas's neck, sending a shiver down his spine before he took a few steps back. "I'll be outside."

It all happened in the scope of a few minutes. Niclas found himself alone in the kitchen, breathing a little heavily. His heart raced; he shook his head a few times, trying to calm his thoughts.

Niclas wasn't exactly inexperienced. He'd dated. Been in a few ill-fated relationships. Most of the men and women he met often tired of his tendency to lose himself in his work, his lifelong passion for historical artefacts, the more mundane, the better. "Tacos. Focus on tacos."

Tacos wouldn't judge him or call him boring. Or weird. Niclas found the plate on the table; Falk had split the food evenly between them. Was this a date, or were they simply friends sharing a meal together?

Was it even sharing if Niclas had been in the shower for part of it and Falk now meandered outside while on the phone?

"It's just tacos. You absolute bampot." Niclas grabbed a bottle of water from the little fridge and sat at the table.

Peering out to his left, Niclas had a lovely view out the window of the fields. Bright green pastures drew his eyes across the farmlands to the sparkling water in the distance. It was easy to breathe in the sea air and pretend nothing out of the ordinary had happened.

Just another treasure-hunting adventure.

Another beautiful location to explore.

He could almost forget that his secret crush had joined him on the adventure. "Tacos. Focus on the tacos."

Maybe if he repeated himself, he'd enjoy the meal and not allow his mind to wander to his conflicted feelings. Probably not, but he had hope. And perhaps, he wouldn't break anything or almost drown again on this trip.

Just eat the tacos.

"This really is a lovely cottage. They were clever to leave the bones of the old barn. The exposed beams, classic whitewashed stone walls." Falk reappeared while Niclas was finishing up the last of his lunch. "These tacos are good, right? Jess suggested the place. Gave me a few, actually."

"Does she still have her bright pink Mohawk?" Niclas had met several of the people who worked with his brother—and Falk. Jessica was one of his favourites. They texted each other every so often. "She hasn't sent me a selfie in a while."

"It's a rainbow at the moment." Falk didn't have a strict dress code for anyone who worked at his private security firm. Izan had told Niclas that they wanted everyone to be comfortable and at ease. "She went green for a while."

"Nice. I'll ask her to send me a photo." Niclas cleaned up the remnants of their lunch. He didn't know what to do with himself. His thoughts and emotions were too chaotic to process. "I'm going to see if I've damaged my detector."

"Nic?"

"Yes?"

"Can I take you out on a date tonight? A proper one. Jess sent me ideas for a few quiet restaurants." Falk stopped him from rushing out of the room. "What do you think?"

"What's a non-proper date?"

"Tacos in the cottage after a morning at the beach." Falk leaned against the kitchen counter, watching Niclas fuss around with the packets from the restaurant. "So, what do you think?"

Niclas stilled his fluttering fingers, glancing over at Falk. "I'd love to go on a date with you."

CHAPTER 10
FALK

YES.

Niclas had said yes to a proper date. It had been a definite yes. And then he'd vanished into his bedroom to tinker with his metal detector.

"Get it together," Falk sternly muttered to himself. He'd stood for an embarrassing length of time with a wide smile on his face. "Let's not chase him off before we've started."

His fingers tingled from the brief touch against Niclas's neck. It was almost embarrassing. Falk had already made a reservation for them, speaking with the owner to ensure they could have a quieter environment.

He wanted them to be able to relax and enjoy the meal. There were numerous occasions when he'd

been at a restaurant with both Ruiz brothers, and Niclas had left owing to the level of noise inside. All he could focus on was the people chatting, the lights, and the smells.

With some luck and cash, Falk hoped to negate the issue before it started. A smaller restaurant was a good idea, along with going at a time outside of the rush. He didn't mind going to the extra effort.

Not for Niclas.

Falk dug into his pocket for his phone when it buzzed. "Evensen."

"Well, aren't we cheerful?"

"Izan." Falk wasn't overly surprised at him calling both Niclas and himself. Overprotective didn't even begin to describe how the elder Ruiz brother could be, at times. "Is anyone managing our clients and teams?"

"I figure they could manage on their own," Izan answered the rhetorical question with a healthy dose of sarcasm. "Is Niclas okay? He seemed off when I spoke with him."

"He's fine. Are you planning to ask the same question every time we speak? I might have to get creative in my responses." Falk had expected some level of concern from Izan. He hadn't anticipated the number of calls. "Don't you trust me?"

"Of course."

"Then trust me when I say he's fine. Stumbled over some rocks. Nothing major. Had a little dip in the sea. No damage aside from maybe being embarrassed." Falk had no idea how Izan might react when he discovered the change in his relationship with Niclas. "So? Anything else?"

"Suppose not," Izan answered after a lengthy silence. "Are *you* off?"

"Off what?"

"You're being narkier than usual."

Falk decided not to poke Izan any further. "No narkier than I normally am. I'm on vacation, yet my phone keeps going off."

"Fine, fine. Just keep him alive." Izan disconnected the call without a goodbye.

Shaking his head, Falk decided Izan was a problem for another day. They'd have to tell him eventually. He wasn't ashamed of his interest in and feelings for Niclas.

But elder siblings, in his experience, could be tricky to deal with. Izan had been protecting Niclas for most of his life. Falk only hoped his friendship with the man helped to smooth things over.

Niclas was an adult and fully capable of taking care of himself. Izan had always tried to not smother his brother. But Falk wasn't sure how that would translate to his engaging in a romantic relationship.

By the time Niclas reappeared from his bedroom, Falk had cleaned the kitchen and gone outside to work out. It was too beautiful to stay indoors for long.

He caught a glimpse of Niclas from the window a few times, checking him out. He made sure not to make it obvious that he'd seen him. *I've still got it.*

"Falk?"

He lifted his head to find Niclas had stepped outside with his gear in hand. "All fixed up?"

"Thought we could check out Tintagel Haven. There's a path down to the beach; I think I've timed the tide correctly. And there's Merlin's cave off to the side." Niclas held up the metal detector in his hand. "Nothing's broken. Checked a few parts. All good."

"All good." Falk took the gear out of his hand and carried it to put in the back of his Range Rover.

Kissing Niclas had been a mistake. Not a mistake. But definitely a mistake. All he could think about was doing it again.

And again.

The drive to Tintagel took no time at all. They arrived to find all the parking spaces in and around the castle jam-packed. Niclas seemed to shrink at the sounds of the tourists swarming around them.

"Like ants."

"Sunburnt, shouting ants," Niclas added to his comment. "Maybe we could go a little further up the coast to Backways Cove? Usually not as crowded. I'm not up to dodging my way through all these people."

"I don't blame you at all." Falk pulled back onto the road and began heading in the direction Niclas pointed out to him. "Never been interested in mingling with the sunburnt and shouting."

Niclas's gaze darted over to him, then back to staring out the window. "They're all a bit overwhelming. People always want to ask questions even when I've got my headphones on."

"Tell you what. I'll hang around behind you, glowering at all of them. It'll put them off." Falk had no doubts even the bravest person would steer clear of him, if only because of his height and his tendency to glower at people. "Or so I'm told."

"Hmm." Niclas leaned his head against the window. "Are we dating?"

"We're going on one tonight, so I'd say we're dating." Falk always kept in mind that Niclas needed him to be clear and precise. He wasn't going to read subtle well; he never had. "Definitely. And if I managed not to chase you off with my bad habits, maybe we'll see where it develops."

"What bad habits?"

"I'm told I'm too particular with how I fold my clothes—and make my bed." Falk smiled when Niclas snickered at him. "Fastidious, I think, is the word your brother threw at me."

"He used the word of the month calendar I got him." Niclas grinned even wider when Falk laughed loudly. "He kept complaining about my using phrases that no one else did. So I figured it might help him expand his vocabulary."

"Why do you love old words so much?"

"It's history. Words mean something. We forget them like the items I find buried in the ground and rivers. There are some magnificent ones." Niclas had this conversation with his brother all the time. Izan never understood. "It's a pity when they vanish from our lexicon. And I don't exactly trot them out constantly. Just find a well-timed sard or bampot is so satisfying."

"Even with the looks you get?"

"People always look at me like my entire being is askew." Niclas shrugged. "At least using old words, they have a legitimate excuse to think I'm wode."

"Wode?"

"Weird. Barmy. Take your pick." Niclas leaned forward to point to the small lane leading down to the closest path to the cove. "Here we are. Not a massively long walk from here. It'll let us work up an appetite for dinner."

Falk could think of a million ways to do that, but he'd settle for another trek to a beach. "Let's go. You try not to fall into the sea, and I'll try not to stumble over a rock."

The cove turned out to be relatively empty. Falk found a place to sit and watch Niclas get lost in his own world. And he did quickly become focused on traversing a grid pattern across the beach.

There was something relaxing about having nothing to do outside of spending time with Niclas. No need to push for conversation. It was a comfortable and pleasant silence.

Not quite silence.

Waves crashed against the rocks. The wind whistled around them. He heard birds periodically sounding overhead.

Maybe Izan had been correct. Not just him, but the rest of his company. They'd all encouraged him to take a break. He threw himself into his work.

There wasn't much else to his life.

In no time, the sun had begun to dip low in the

sky. Their stomachs had begun to rumble. Falk easily followed the directions the restaurant owner had given him when he'd called to set things up for their date.

They'd promised him a private space with a great view. Falk wondered if anywhere along the Cornish coast came with a bad one. The drive was quiet again.

Not uncomfortably so.

The restaurant was a cosy little space with a large bed & breakfast. The owner had set them up on the balcony of one of their rooms. It was intimate and quiet.

A perfect first date.

Delicious food, a spectacular sunset, and a peaceful drive back to the cottage. Falk didn't want the night to end. Neither did Niclas, from the way they'd both found themselves standing outside, watching each other.

His fingers itched to reach out for Niclas. Falk didn't want to push him. They'd kissed already; surely the end of a first date warranted another kiss?

Falk stalked closer to Niclas. "How'd I do for our first night out?"

"Good. Moon and stars are watching. Careful." Niclas leaned against the side of the cottage, head tilted up to stare at the night sky. "Thank you for going to the—"

"It wasn't any extra effort. I'm just glad you were able to enjoy yourself." Falk refused to be thanked for doing the bare minimum to make his life easier. Instead, he rested his hand on the wall beside Niclas's head. "You ever kissed under the stars on a breezy Cornish night?"

"No. That's an oddly specific question." Niclas shifted in front of him. His fingers went up to grip the lapels of Falk's jacket, tugging him forward with impressive strength. "I'm open to changing the answer to my question."

Their first kisses hadn't been tentative, but more exploratory. This wasn't. Falk found every taste of Niclas left him wanting more.

"What the hell is going on?"

Falk jolted back from Niclas. He had no idea how long they'd been kissing by the cottage. He withdrew his hands from underneath Niclas's shirt and turned to find Izan storming towards them. "What are you doing in Cornwall?"

"Not the question that needs answering. What the hell are you doing with my brother?" Izan generally kept his cool, but Falk could see him spiralling out of control. "What—"

"Just stop it. Stop." Niclas cut his brother off midsentence with a shout, leaving Falk and Izan a little stunned. He couldn't recall ever seeing the younger Ruiz lose his temper. "We've had a perfect night, and you've mucked with my memory of the end of it."

While they watched, Niclas fumbled with the keys to the cottage. He muttered curses until he managed to get inside. The door slammed shut behind him with a heavy thud.

"Damn it, Iz."

"Let him go for now. He needs to sit by himself to calm down. Losing his temper usually winds up in him having a shutdown." Izan caught Falk by the arm to stop him from following. "I shouldn't have shouted."

"No, you shouldn't have. Ruined a nice night. Our first date." Falk folded his arms across his chest. He had nothing to be sorry over. He had nothing to feel guilty about, so he refused to allow the emotion to take hold of him. "We're consenting adults."

"You're right. You're right. I... Sometimes it's hard not to worry about him. He's been hurt so many times." Izan scratched the back of his neck. "So, old friend, how long have you been in love with my brother?"

"Long enough."

"Why the hell haven't you asked him out before?" Izan was suddenly irate on behalf of his brother for a wholly different reason.

"You were just about five seconds away from throwing a punch at me for kissing him—and now you're upset that I didn't do it sooner?"

"It's called pivoting."

"You're such an absolute wanker." Falk grinned when Izan shoved him. "Pivot. Nic was right; you're using the word-a-day calendar that he bought you."

"I'm… What? What calendar?"

CHAPTER 11
NICLAS

THE SILENT RUSHING OF SOUND IN HIS HEAD HADN'T stopped. Niclas retreated to his room, closing the door and kicking off his shoes. He also yanked off his shirt when it felt as though the fabric were stifling the air out of him.

Sitting on the floor, Niclas dragged over one of his organising bins. He pried off the lid with a little effort. His fingers didn't want to cooperate with him.

Organising his treasures had always helped to calm him. Niclas hunted for one of the soft bristle brushes from his tool kit and took it. It allowed him to focus his mind.

Picking up one of the badges he'd found previously—it was likely medieval, probably a lead alloy

of some sort—he handled it with gloves, tracing the moulded beadwork on the outer rim.

It was soothing.

Stroke.

Stroke.

Stroke.

The fine, soft bristles delicately swiped over the inner cross. Each arm was decorated. All connected within a circle to make up the badge that would've been worn on clothing.

It was almost ritualistic. Niclas allowed his mind to drift while he cleaned any remaining sand and dirt off the intricate design. The buzzing under his skin faded away with each stroke.

Halfway through the container, Niclas found his legs starting to protest the cramped position. He packed away his tools and artefacts. It took a few minutes for him to clean the sand off the floor.

He walked around barefoot to make sure he'd gotten all of it. *Sard.* It was gritty. Grimacing at the sensation, Niclas did a second sweep up, only to go over the floor a third time.

There.

His bed beckoned, but his stomach rumbled. Niclas snuck out of his room into the kitchen, hoping to avoid waking Falk up. He wondered if Izan had left already.

Niclas opened the fridge to find a sandwich already waiting for him. Ham and cheese with toasted bread brushed with olive oil. It was perfect. He found a Post-it Note on the plate next to it. "Sorry I ruined your first date."

"And I am."

"Death's head upon a mop-stick."

"I'm sorry, what?" Izan had flipped on the light, darting forward to catch the plate when it slipped from Niclas's hands. "Learn a new phrase?"

"Isn't it brilliant?"

"It is, actually. Death's head upon a mop-stick?" Izan accepted half of the sandwich when Niclas offered it.

"Dates probably from the 1700s." Niclas had read it while combing through old plays and poems by Edmund John Eyre. "Stuck in my mind. It's quite a visual."

"Thought you might be hungry when you'd worked off your stress." Izan dug into the fridge and came out with two bottles of water. "Here."

"Ravenous."

"I am sorry, Nic. I shouldn't have reacted…"

"Like a bampot."

"If that means arsehole, then yes." Izan joined him at the little table in the kitchen with a bag of crisps in hand. He nudged the plate closer to Niclas. "So, Falk. My best mate."

"Yes." Niclas's stomach churned. He set down the sandwich without taking a bite, suddenly not quite so hungry. "Yes, he is."

"And you fancy him?"

Niclas scraped his thumbnail across the crust of his sandwich, slowly building a pile of crumbs on the plate. "I…"

"Nic? I'm not angry."

"Fancied him for an embarrassingly long time." Niclas pushed his plate away before he massacred the entire sandwich. "I didn't believe he returned the sentiment. I'm just your poxy younger brother."

"Niclas." Izan groaned before reaching over to place a hand on his shoulder. "Pretty sure he 'returns the sentiment.' How do you really feel about him?"

"Hertis rote," Niclas mumbled.

"Sorry? You've lost me."

"Middle English, if I recall correctly. It means my heart's root." Niclas patted his hand over his heart. "Don't tell him I said that. He'll laugh."

"He wouldn't." Izan nudged the plate back over to

him. "Eat. Also, if Grizz does laugh, I'll kick his arse."

"Izan." Niclas glanced briefly up at his brother. "You don't mind?"

"Surprised. I was surprised more than upset with you." Izan shifted forward in his chair. He sounded serious, so Niclas believed him. "What matters to me is that you're happy. Are you?"

"I would've been happier if you hadn't caught me bussing him under the stars." Niclas grabbed his sandwich, taking a large bite since his stomach had settled. "The humiliation."

"Bussing."

"Snogging? Kissing? What do you plebeians use these days?" Niclas grinned when Izan flicked a crisp at him. "I'm not delving into the details with you."

"Good, I have innocent ears."

"How are your ears innocent? You went to war. They've heard worse than my gaining some mild carnal knowledge of Falk." Niclas ignored his brother choking on a sip of water and continued eating his sandwich. "Wait. That was a joke, wasn't it?"

They ate in silence for a few minutes. Niclas was reminded of all the late nights he'd struggled with his studies. Izan had stayed up with him when he'd been home from military service.

"I'll take the sofa. You should get some rest." Izan grabbed both of their now empty plates.

"You're staying?"

"Just for a few days."

Niclas glared suspiciously at his brother's chin. "Why?"

"You wouldn't throw your poor brother out into the cold. It's such a long drive back to the office." Izan chuckled when Niclas sighed loudly. "I'll behave myself."

"I don't believe you." Niclas trudged out of the kitchen. "But I'm too tired to figure out what you mean."

CHAPTER 12
FALK

Finding Izan on the sofa had been unexpected; he'd anticipated him already being on his way home. Not unpleasant but not necessarily welcome either. Falk mentally prepared himself for a potentially trying day.

Izan might have accepted his relationship with Niclas, but he was still a protective older brother. One who'd definitely enjoy being able to tease one of his friends. Falk had no doubts his patience would be tested.

Falk had coffee brewing when Izan dragged himself into the kitchen to join him. "Morning."

"I've been thinking."

"Always a terrifying opening to any conversa-

tion." Falk grabbed three mugs out of the cupboard. They were all going to need to be caffeinated. He hunted in the fridge for eggs and bacon, planning a simple breakfast. "What terrors have you decided to inflict upon me?"

"When you defile my brother—"

"What the actual fuck?" Falk choked on his own saliva. He glanced over to find Izan practically wheezing with laughter. "You're such a wanker."

"Help. I can't breathe." Izan leaned against the counter, holding his side and trying to slow down his laughter. "Your face was an absolute picture. I should've taken a video for Jess."

"For someone who can't breathe, you're doing a fair amount of nattering." Falk had the coffee machine going, so he moved on to cracking eggs and whisking them up for easy omelettes. "You'll give your brother a complex if you're not careful. And we're both asexual."

"I wouldn't give him a complex. And I recognise that defiling might be different with you." Izan managed to calm himself down. "I'll encourage whatever and whoever makes him happy. Break his heart, and they'll never find your body."

A loud bang interrupted their banter. Niclas stumbled into the kitchen a second later, rubbing his elbow and grumbling about walls moving. He was adorable when grumpy, despite it not being his usual state of mind.

"Did you try opening your eyes?"

"Fopdoddle." Niclas glowered at his brother before returning his attention to the state of his elbow. "Nothing humorous about a funny bone."

"You could say it's humerus," Izan teased.

"Wrong bone."

"Really?"

"I mean, technically? Isn't it at the end?" Niclas was still a bit bleary-eyed while he reached for one of the mugs of coffee that Falk had just poured. He held his hand out to his brother. "Phone."

Izan chuckled but complied. He unlocked his phone and held it out to Niclas. "If you stopped forgetting yours, you could do research on it without waiting for someone else's."

"Fopdoddle."

"Stop calling me a fool." Izan accepted the mug that Falk handed to him. "It ruins the joke when you dig too deeply into it."

"The elbow is made up of three bones—one is the humerus." Niclas tossed the phone back to his brother. "Joke only mildly disrupted."

"Mildly."

"Fully since the funny bone isn't even a bone to begin with." Niclas grinned when Izan launched into a playful rant about ruining jokes and taking things literally.

Making breakfast, Falk enjoyed listening to the brothers playfully snipe at each other. Izan knew how to toe the line without either confusing or hurting Niclas. He wondered how long it had taken Izan to learn those edges.

Niclas was clever. Brilliant, even. But he often missed jokes. He didn't grasp things in ways one might expect.

And Falk never wanted to be someone who dimmed the light inside of him—even accidentally.

"Oi, Viking, where's our breakfast?" Izan banged his fist against the table. "Eggs. Eggs."

"Could you, if at all possible, bellow less?" Niclas appeared a few seconds away from drowning himself in his mug of coffee. "We are not at a fish market."

"Eggs," Izan murmured quietly.

"I regret not sending him home last night." Niclas wrapped both hands around the mug. He bent forward, allowing his hair to shield his eyes. "I enjoy history. I do not enjoy the chaperone aspect of romantic liaisons."

"Are we going hunting?"

"We?" Niclas glanced between Falk and Izan. "I'm going to Lundy Bay. Not supposed to be next on the list, but I've crossed out a few of the coves."

"Why?" Izan exchanged a concerned glance with Falk when Niclas shrugged in response. "Nic? You've planned this carefully for months and months. You've had a map with pins in specific locations on a wall in your living room. Why would you drop them now?"

"Marcus texted me this morning. Charlene's managed to get permits for some of the coves and beaches on the same days I had them." Niclas murmured a thank-you when Falk set a plate in front of him. "I can make my life easier by avoiding her. She wants a reaction; I won't give her one if I'm not there."

"Do you—"

"I don't want to converse about it." Niclas shovelled eggs and two strips of bacon onto a slice of toast. He smashed another on top and then moved away from the table. "At all."

Falk set down Izan's plate. "I'll talk to him."

"I—"

"Iz. Let me." Falk grabbed his coffee mug along with Niclas's. He found him gathering his gear while taking angry bites out of his sandwich. "There are times, in war, that your best option is retreat. Not every battle has to be fought."

"I was never aware I was fighting a battle. Feel like a right fopdoddle." Niclas shoved a container into his backpack. "Just thought she was being sarcastic. Not trying to wreck my work."

"Nothing wrong with thinking the best of people."

"There is when they take advantage of my naiveté." Niclas picked at the bit of egg that had dropped to his shirt.

"Says more about her than about you."

"And yet." Niclas flopped down on the edge of the bed. "Throughout my school and career, I've done double or triple the work just to feel as though I'm… normal. Worthwhile."

Falk resisted the urge to offer some platitude that might make Niclas feel dismissed. "I hear you. It's not right. The world doesn't even attempt to make life accessible for you."

"I manage."

"You do. But your effort and work don't equate to your worth." Falk reached out to stop Niclas from yanking on the laces of his boots. "Slow down. We're all worth far more than the sum total of our accomplishments, Nic."

Niclas shrugged. "Sometimes it feels as though the world only finds worth in autistics when we're geniuses. It's a load of codswallop."

"Agreed."

Niclas covered Falk's hand. His fingers nimbly danced over his before releasing him and returning to attempting to untie the knot he'd created in the laces. "Thank you. Not always easy to talk to people about my frustrations. They either placate me or try to relate a little too hard when all I really want is to feel heard. To feel as if someone is genuinely listening without trying to solve the problem for me."

"Always here to listen." Falk was painfully aware of Izan in the next room, waiting for them. "So, where are we going today?"

"Lundy Bay." Niclas finished changing out slippers for his hiking boots. "It will hopefully be Charlene free, and if we're lucky, Izan won't linger."

"He will." Falk smiled when Niclas sighed heavily. "He loves you."

"It doesn't make him any less annoying."

"Family can be annoying and loving in equal measure." Falk couldn't help but reach out to run his fingers through Niclas's mussed-up hair. "He has to go back to the office eventually. And I'm not going to be scared off by Izan. Nothing he says or does will deter me from wanting a second date, a third, and a fourth. And he certainly won't change my mind on needing another chance at a goodnight kiss."

"Just a goodnight kiss?"

"It's a perfect place to start."

CHAPTER 13
NICLAS

Lundy Bay.

Not his favourite spot. Niclas had never had much luck along this particular stretch of the Cornish coastline. It was partly why he hadn't minded too much when Charlene poked her nose into his trip.

As much as her motivations aggravated him, Niclas was happy to allow her to have the rockiest beaches, which rarely offered much in the way of treasure. Lundy Bay had a few sections at low tide that were ripe for the picking.

Once they'd found a spot at the Lundy Bay car park, Niclas led his brother and Falk to the coastal path. It eventually veered off toward the beach, ending at wooden stairs. Fortunately, they found the beach relatively empty.

Niclas took his metal detector from Izan, who'd insisted on carrying it for him. "Not sure how you'll entertain yourself while I'm scanning the beach. Please don't hover."

"I'd never." Izan dodged out of the way when Niclas kicked sand at him. "Peace, peace. What does Falk do while you're hunting for treasure?"

"He doesn't bother me." Niclas grabbed his headphones out of his bag. He got his detector turned on and ready to go. "You're not here."

"I mean, technically…." Izan trailed off when Falk grabbed him by the shoulder. "We'll be over there."

Not even looking in the direction his brother pointed, Niclas reached into his backpack for his notebook. He'd jotted down grids for each location. A general guide for himself to not only know where to start but to be able to mark off areas he'd searched and keep track of ones he hadn't.

With the grid set in his mind, Niclas left his backpack on a large rock near his brother. He adjusted the volume on his headset and started the first sweep with the detector. It was challenging with an audience.

The first ten minutes were a waste. Niclas had to scan the same area three times. He kept glancing towards his brother and Falk, wondering what they were talking about.

His anxiety told him they were talking about him. Logically, Niclas knew it wouldn't be anything terrible, even if they were. It took several minutes to calm and focus his mind.

With his little shovel dangling from his belt, Niclas went to work. He scanned half of the beach without finding anything. Not a massive surprise; Cornish coves were a gamble, since so many had come before to try to find treasures.

A lot of the beaches were picked clean. But he still discovered enough to bring him back every couple of years. And even with tourists packing the area, there was some measure of peace for him.

It was disheartening to have not found anything at all. He was jolted out of his thoughts when a hand rested on his shoulder. Falk held out a water bottle.

"Hydrate," Falk said after Niclas had pulled the headphones off and looped them around his neck. "You've been going for over an hour. Drink some water."

Niclas frowned at the water hovering in front of his face before finally taking it. He propped his metal detector against his side and chugged half the bottle down. "Most obliged."

"Oh, oh, fine. I see how it is. Let him help you and interrupt your work. But if I do it, you get all huffy and tell me I'm a bothering pillock." Izan laughed when Niclas chucked a small pebble at him. "I can see who you like more."

"Well, yes, I want to nursle him."

"Nursle." Izan narrowed his eyes. "Swear you make this shite up to mess with my head."

"Old word for nuzzling." Niclas drank more of the water before offering the bottle back to Falk. He glanced in the direction of his brother. "Would you prefer fornicate?"

"I…" Izan strolled away, muttering to himself. "You don't even—never mind."

"As I suspected." Niclas eased his headphones back on, nodded to Falk, and returned to scanning the beach. *Fornicate. Old words roll off the tongue.* "He is so easy to rile up."

It was one of the things Niclas enjoyed most about reviving forgotten words. They often had a different cadence to them. They were fun.

Fun wasn't a strong enough word.

His obsession had started with Niclas's very first task at the museum. He'd culled through old letters and manuscripts. Some of the paper had been so brittle and delicate.

It had taken him a year and a half to work through the donated documents. So many words had leapt off the page at him. He'd created a journal where he jotted down the ones he'd never heard in the hopes of one day being able to write a book of his own about them.

A dictionary of the forgotten. The market for it might be small, but Niclas had learned others were as passionate as he when it came to living language. So it was a side project he added to whenever he came across a new word.

The rarer and more obscure, the better. Pushing thoughts of his passion project to the side, Niclas focused on listening to his detector. He gave himself another hour before it was time to move on.

He'd found nothing. Four hours. It wasn't a waste of time, since he never felt it was pointless. He could cross off a location, if nothing else.

Niclas carefully went over the last part of the beach. The tide had begun to come in. He'd managed to time his search almost perfectly. "Well, Lundy, you've failed me again."

The words were just out of his mouth when his metal detector beeped. Niclas ran the coil over the spot a few times from a different direction, then hit the button to pinpoint the target. He crouched down, pulling the little trowel off his belt.

"Find something interesting?" Falk came over to join him, crouching down beside him.

"I have found…." Niclas finished clearing off the hole. He reached down and triumphantly held up his prize. "A squashed beer can."

"Well, if nothing else, you've done your part for the planet today." Falk took the can from him. "We'll find a rubbish bin on the way to lunch. You ready to go? Think Izan's getting antsy."

"Izan wants you to know that there is no fornicating or nuzzling in front of him." His brother made a rude gesture at his old friend. "Have we picked a spot for lunch?"

"We don't fornicate. Nuzzling is definitely on the menu." Falk winked at Niclas, who grinned.

"There are a few places at Polzeath." Niclas had made a list of potential restaurants, though most of the time, he preferred to pack a lunch if he remembered. "Maybe a sandwich place? Something light since I've another beach I want to visit. Iz? When are you leaving?"

"I'm hurt. Still trying to get rid of me so soon?" Izan clutched his chest dramatically. "If I leave before lunch, who's going to chaperone your lunch and ensure your reputation isn't ruined?"

"A chaperone? Now who's the one being archaic?" Niclas rolled his eyes at his brother's antics. "If you give me indigestion because you're oddly over-dramatic about Falk and I potentially canoodling, I'm going to be very wroth with you."

"Wroth. Honestly." Izan grabbed Niclas's back-pack from him. He hefted it over his shoulder. "C'mon, you two, I'll buy lunch."

CHAPTER 14

FALK

Lunch had been simple. They'd found a little café that put together sandwiches, chips, fruit, and drinks for them. Niclas had suggested a quiet spot near Polzeath Beach.

"We've got a client issue." Izan waved Falk over to the side. They left Niclas sitting on a bench and went to discuss. "Edwin texted me earlier. He said they're demanding at least three more people on their team for a weekend business trip."

"For what?" Falk didn't hear Izan's answer. A strange gurgling sound caught his attention. "What—"

Cutting himself off, Falk spun around to find Niclas on his feet. He was bent over the bench in

obvious distress. The gurgling noise was coming from his throat.

"Fuck." Falk raced over. He got an arm around Niclas, bending him further forward and pounding his hand against his back five times. "Breathe, damn it."

Niclas choked and coughed before water spewed out of his mouth. He gripped the bench, gasping for air. "I'm okay."

"Just take it easy and slow." Falk kept his arm around Niclas's upper body, supporting him while he inhaled deeply and desperately. "That's it. Focus on breathing."

"Hit my back again," Niclas wheezed.

A lengthy career as a combat medic kept Falk calm. He ignored Izan, who was now hovering behind them. Instead, he leaned back a little to smack the palm of his hand between Niclas's shoulder blades another five times.

He paused, waiting. Niclas wheezed and choked. Another five strikes before a chunk of food and more water came out of him.

Niclas sank back into Falk's arms, gasping for air again. He hiccupped and then burped while rubbing his hand against his chest. "Sarding grapes. Ridiculous fruit. Never eating them ever again."

"Slowly does it. Rest your voice." Falk tried to

guide Niclas down onto the bench. He was up a second later.

"Nope, not sitting." Niclas stayed bent over, gripping the back of the bench for support. "Sarding grapes."

"So you said." Falk rubbed his hand over Niclas's back. He winced at the painful-sounding, hoarse cough. "Shallow breaths. Just get some air into your lungs."

"Think I'm ready to try water again. Maybe it'll help." Niclas grabbed the water bottle his brother held out to him. He took a small sip and then immediately coughed violently. "Nope, nope, bad plan. Not ready."

Falk continued patting Niclas's back until the water was out. He exchanged a worried glance with Izan. "Think you can sit down now?"

Niclas seemed hesitant to move, not that anyone could blame him. He allowed Falk to help ease him down onto the bench. He shifted back a little. "I don't know if I'm uneasy because of remembered panic or if I'm still struggling."

"Don't talk for a little while. Just keep going with the slow breathing. You've had a scare—give yourself time to recover." Falk placed a hand on Niclas's shoulder and massaged gently. "You're okay."

Izan sank down to the ground in front of them. He seemed to be breathing almost as heavily as his brother had been. "For fuck's sake, Nic. Think you scared years off my life."

"I hate grapes." Niclas settled back into silence. He glowered at the fruit that remained of his lunch.

"How about we take those out of your hands?" Falk nodded to Izan, who grabbed the packet of fruit and put it back inside the bag. "You focus on your breathing, okay?"

"Sarding grapes." Niclas continually repeated the phrase under his breath.

"Yes, damn the grapes." Izan hadn't moved from where he sat on the sand. He kept glancing over at his brother as if expecting to see an injury for him to take care of. "You going to live?"

Niclas rolled his eyes. "Breathing seems an excellent start."

After a few more minutes, Niclas took the water bottle from Falk again. He hesitantly sipped the barest amount. Falk remained tense, ready to jump into action if necessary, but this time the liquid went down without an issue.

"Slowly," Izan encouraged.

"If I go any slower, the water will reverse up my

throat." Niclas managed another measure of water. Then another. Then another. "Progress."

"You scared the absolute shite out of me." Izan shook his head ruefully. "Honestly. What the hell happened?"

"Not sure." Niclas sipped more water. His voice was a little shaky, and his fingers visibly trembled around the bottle. Falk sat on the bench beside him and looped an arm around his shoulders. "Noshing on the grapes. A part of one got stuck in my throat. I drank to try and get it to go down, but then I couldn't breathe."

There was a lengthy silence. Falk's arm rested lightly around Niclas's shoulders. He didn't want to apply too much pressure or weight, but his presence did seem to help calm the shaking.

Falk dug through the bag beside him on the bench and found a small bar of chocolate. "Take a bite and suck on the chocolate. Get a little sugar in you to combat the shock."

Niclas was hesitant to take the chocolate but finally did. "Not sure I want to try eating anything at the moment."

"Just a little," Falk encouraged.

Sipping more water, Niclas held the chocolate in his hand. He finally popped it in his mouth. Falk hoped the sugar would help steady him—and it was less likely to cause his throat to seize up again out of fear.

"You're going to be tired. It's perfectly normal. You've had a terrifying shock. And being repeatedly whacked on the back by a Viking won't have helped. How about we head back to the cottage?" Izan got to his feet, brushing the sand off his jeans. Falk could see the worry etched on his face. "I'll swing by the shops to fix up dinner for us. And don't worry; I won't be invading your holiday for much longer, just another night. I'll head out soon enough."

"I'm okay." Niclas tipped the bottle back, taking a much larger gulp than he had previously. "See? I'm okay."

"Humour me, okay?" Izan grabbed the bags that had contained their lunch. "I'll… deal with this."

They watched him stalk away toward the path leading to the car park. Falk rarely saw his best friend so out of sorts. It was clear Izan didn't want to bleed his worry and fears all over Niclas.

Niclas took a few deep breaths. He counted them quietly while staring out at the returning tide. "He's always good in the middle of a crisis but tends to need a moment after."

"Fairly certain anyone would want a second to

recover after the scare we just had." Falk had a feeling he'd be hearing the gurgling noise Niclas had made in his nightmares for weeks. "How are you feeling?"

"Still a little shaky." Niclas held up his hand to demonstrate. He dropped it back to his leg and continued his slow breathing for a few minutes. "Not sure I've ever been so terrified in my life."

"Same."

"You went to war."

"Yes, and I had moments that left me with anxiety and post-traumatic stress. But it's been a while since I've been terrified for someone I love." Falk saw no reason to hide his feelings for Niclas. They'd known each other for years. *Why waste more time?* Life was incredibly cruel and short when it wanted to be. He draped his arm around Niclas's shoulders again, drawing him into his body for a hug and turning his head to brush a kiss against his temple. "All the training in the world doesn't guarantee I'm going to be successful. There's always a heavy dose of fear that I'll be too late."

"You weren't." Niclas leaned into him further. "I'm breathing. Did you say 'someone you love'?"

"I did." Falk refused to back down now when he'd wanted to be able to say the words for so long.

"Promise me something, since you love me?" Niclas canted his head to the side to look at Falk's nose. "Since you love me like I love you."

"Yes? What?"

"If I die by grape? Lie. Come up with a better story, for my sake?" Niclas stayed serious for all of a second before snickering. "I mean it. I do not want to go into the beyond with people laughing at my funeral."

"Death by grape." Falk snorted.

"Sarding grapes."

"Come on. Let's get back to the vehicle." Falk got to his feet and pulled Niclas up with him. They made their way to the car park.

It had been a trying day. Falk thought Niclas wanted nothing more than to be at home with his things surrounding him in his own space. But instead, he was in Cornwall with his brother and his… something. They hadn't quite quantified their relationship yet.

And today was not going to be the day for them to do so.

His fingers continued to tremble for a long time even after they'd gotten inside the vehicle. Falk had turned the heat on, which helped. He knew the body could have a delayed reaction, particularly for Niclas.

No matter how hard he tried to make it otherwise.

Niclas tapped his fingers on the door handle. He leaned his head against the window and closed his eyes against the blur of the passing scenery. Laughter bubbled up out of him, causing Falk to glance over at him. "Grapes."

"Pardon?"

"Grapes. A grape. Water and grape. I almost died because of half-formed wine." Niclas couldn't help snickering.

"Fairly confident there's more to wine than water and grapes." Falk chuckled. He reached over to turn down the heat when Niclas had finally stopped shivering. "Are we still moving to a new location tomorrow?"

"I've got the cottages booked." Niclas was no longer shivering, but he looked like he'd run a marathon. "I'm so… weary."

"Near-death experiences will do that to you." Falk reached over to rest his hand on Niclas's arm. "Why not take the rest of the day off? Try again tomorrow."

Niclas laughed again. It had a hint of hysteria at the end, but Falk was kind enough not to comment. "You said love."

"I did." Falk glanced over at him while they were stopped at a junction. He rested his hand against the back of Niclas's neck; his fingers stroked soothingly. "Fairly certain you responded in kind."

"I did." Niclas couldn't quite mimic the deep timbre of Falk's voice. He leaned into his touch for a second. "I'm starving but also petrified of attempting to eat."

"We'll start with soup or something small. Chew slowly."

"Masticate until it's nothing but mush?"

"Masticate." Falk coughed a few times. "Not what I thought you said."

"Masti…." Niclas snorted, then cackled with laughter. "*Honestly.*"

CHAPTER 15
NICLAS

Laughter was supposedly good for the soul. Niclas could admit chuckling with Falk had done wonders for his mood. The heat in the vehicle and Falk's touch had soothed him as well.

They'd arrived at the cottage to find Izan hadn't returned yet. Niclas wanted nothing more than to climb into bed for a few hours. However, he was afraid to attempt a full meal, considering a grape had almost had him walking into the light.

"I'll carry your bags."

"I can manage," Niclas immediately insisted. He reconsidered a moment later when even lifting a bag sounded too much. "I…"

"Appreciate the help, but I am as horrible as my brother at accepting?" Falk offered a kind smile

before picking up the bags himself. "Beautiful afternoon out. Nice breeze. Why don't you lean into the British cure-all? Tea in the garden."

There was a sweet concern to the way Falk guided him through getting his things into his room in the cottage and then outside into the fresh air. He slouched onto the wooden bench situated under an oak tree. A warm mug of tea was placed in his hands a few minutes later, but then he'd been left to his thoughts, potentially not the greatest idea in the world.

His thoughts and emotions were all over the place. It seemed overdramatic. He was clearly fine, but he still remembered the panic setting in when he couldn't breathe.

Nothing Niclas had done had helped. He'd had zero control over regaining the ability to breathe. It had been one of the most frightening things to have happened to him ever.

The garden was on a slight slant. The tree stood at the top, allowing him to lounge back against the trunk while enjoying the spectacular view all the way down to the cliffs and the sea beyond.

"You scared me." Izan had stepped noisily through the garden, giving him fair warning of his presence.

Niclas had enjoyed his calm, breezy time in the garden in relative silence. "Frightful experience for all involved."

"Never been good with being helpful. It's not a comfortable sensation for someone trained to remain calm under pressure." Izan sat beside him on the bench. He set a Freddo on Niclas's knee. It had been the go-to chocolate treat whenever Niclas had a bad day as a child. "For when you're ready to attempt eating again."

"I managed water." Niclas peeled the wrapper open slowly. He stared down at the chocolate. "This shouldn't be frightening."

"Have a tiny bite. I promise to pound you on the back if it gets stuck." Izan stretched his legs out in front of him. "Beautiful here."

Niclas nibbled on the bottom of the Freddo. He half-expected his throat to seize up like it had when he'd tried drinking water initially. "More than beautiful."

"I'll be heading out in an hour. I brought soup. Thought your throat might appreciate it." Izan fished another Freddo out of his pocket. He tore the wrapper and popped the entire chocolate into his mouth, grinning when Niclas grimaced at him. "What?"

"No one wants or needs to see the process of

mastication." He rolled his eyes when Izan snickered. "At all. Ever."

They teased each other for a few more seconds, but Niclas could see his brother turning serious. He grew nervous in the ensuing silence. His fingers began to itch, causing him to rub them on his jeans repeatedly until Izan reached out to grab his wrist.

"You're not in trouble. I'm not about to go off on you." Izan let go of his hand. He dug out two more Freddos, tossing one to Niclas and keeping the last one for himself. "Falk's always been good under pressure. Both of us have. We trained for it. Never saw him go quite so pale as when we heard you fucking gurgling like a water fountain."

"I'm…"

"You're perfectly okay. I'm aware. Grizz cares about you. I've seen him less shaken while dealing with wounds on a fellow soldier." Izan held his hand up when Niclas went to ask a question. "Not my stories to tell. It's harder to be detached when it's someone you love."

"Izan."

"All I'm saying is I want dibs on being the best man at the wedding." Izan laughed loudly when Niclas shoved him off the bench. "Fine, fine. I see how it is. I should get on the road if I want to get back to the office at a decent time. Try not to elope on me."

"*Izan.*"

"Yeah, yeah. I love you too." Izan dragged Niclas up into a fierce hug and then sauntered off, whistling the wedding march far too loudly. "Stay away from grapes."

"Bampot."

"Taking that as a compliment." Izan waved before disappearing into the cottage.

Brothers.

With his brother gone, Niclas returned to enjoying the peace and quiet. He stayed in the garden for a while longer. He'd always needed more time to process things life threw at him. Almost dying definitely required more than the usual amount.

The sun was starting to set when Falk made his way out of the cottage to join him. He offered Niclas an oversized mug of soup and then sat beside him. Their legs were pressed together while they sipped.

"Have I mentioned how pleased I am you foisted yourself into my vacation?" Niclas drank the soup as slowly as possible. Part of him was still worried about choking again. "And not just because you saved my life."

"It's the kissing, right?"

"Maybe not *just* the kissing." Niclas leaned into Falk, who draped his arm across the back of the bench. "It's an enjoyable part of the equation."

"Kissing is an enjoyable part of the equation. Put that on a T-shirt." Falk set his mug on the bench. His legs were stretched out in front of him, longer than Niclas's. "How high on the list? Top two?"

"Three. Right underneath your first aid knowledge and chauffeuring me around in something larger than my Mini." Niclas stretched his legs out as well, nudging Falk lightly with his foot. "Maybe top two."

CHAPTER 16
FALK

"I SET SOMETHING UP INSIDE THE COTTAGE FOR US." Falk had waited until they finished their soup and the sun had set to interrupt the calm in the garden. "A second date, of sorts."

"Oh?" Niclas carefully folded and unfolded the Freddo wrapper in his fingers. "What are we doing?"

Falk watched him out of the corner of his eye. He knew from past experience that Niclas didn't enjoy surprises. "I've got a movie trilogy for us to enjoy. Snacks. Lots of snacks, and I'll get a fresh pot of tea for us."

"Movies?"

"*The Mummy*." Falk smiled when Niclas immediately perked up. "Thought your favourite comfort film might be a good choice."

"Definite favourite." Niclas shoved the wrapper into his pocket and got to his feet. "What sort of snacks?"

"Ones that hopefully don't come with near-death experiences." Falk stood up. He stretched his arms above his head and then straightened his shirt. "Izan purchased them while getting everything for the soup. I sent him a list."

"He voluntarily purchased things for our date?"

"He's coming around to the idea of us together." Falk thought Izan was likely relieved to have someone he trusted dating his younger brother.

"You mean he likes you better than my last boyfriend?" Niclas followed him into the cottage. He glanced around, noticing all the faery lights inside were turned on. "You've set up quite an atmosphere."

"Lights, camera, action?" Falk teased. He knew the day had been a rough one for Niclas. "Your brother raided the entire snack aisle. Think we've got every flavour of crisp available, plus a variety of pastries from the bakery."

The array of treats was impressive. Falk wondered how much Izan had shelled out for the unhealthy feast. Niclas grabbed the Roast Beef Monster Munch bag and settled himself on the middle of the sofa, leaving plenty of room for Falk to join him on either side.

"Comfortable?"

"Immeasurably." Niclas popped one of the crisps into his mouth and then chewed as slowly as was humanly possible. He blushed a little when Falk continued watching him. "Better safe than sorry. Sarding grapes."

Grabbing drinks for both of them, Falk joined him on the sofa. He left a little space between them, allowing Niclas to decide how close he wanted to be. It wasn't long before the younger man inched over the rest of the way.

They were halfway through the first movie and had made a decent dint in the snacks when Niclas slumped against him. His head rested against Falk, who lifted his arm to wrap around him. He adjusted the volume a little.

"This was my non-sexual awakening." Niclas gestured towards the screen where three of the major characters in the movie were arguing. "I watched with a uni friend. They waxed poetic about Evie, Rick, and Ardeth. It was when they realised they were bisexual —and I was far more interested in the books and cartouche. I enjoyed Rick and Ardeth aesthetically, but it didn't fire up my loins."

"Fire up your loins?" Falk chuckled.

"They're aesthetically pleasing, as I said, but… I wasn't fondling myself at the thought of them." Niclas lifted his head when Falk burst out laughing. "When was your non-sexual awakening?"

"In university, realising I fancied a friend but didn't want more when he did. But I think it was in the military when I began to understand myself." Falk cringed at the memory. "It was a while before I was able to accept myself. I tried to fit myself into a mould for longer than I should've."

"It wasn't my brother, was it?" Niclas glanced at him, horrified.

"No, Nic, I have never once had any form of attraction to your brother aside from him being one of my closest friends." Falk shook his head. He grimaced at the thought of it, then laughed. "We should never mention this conversation to him. He'll take the mickey for the rest of our lives."

"Fair point." Niclas leaned back against him. "My non-celebrity awakening came when I met one of Izan's friends. Tall, handsome grizzly Viking of a man."

"Nic."

"I speak the truth," Niclas stated dramatically.

"Now hush, Evie's drunken ramble is one of my favourite parts."

Settling back against the cushions, Falk sipped his drink while watching Niclas. He was quoting along with the movie almost word for word. It was sweet and endearing.

Niclas had obviously watched *The Mummy* a million times. Falk found himself enjoying it all the more for how much his companion did. He hoped there were many more evenings in the future like this one.

"We've danced around the topic, but you're okay with there never being anything more than kissing, right?" Niclas spoke so quietly his voice was almost drowned out by the movie. "I love cuddling. Being close with you. But I've never been interested in all the rest of the sexual aspects of a relationship."

"Neither have I," Falk was quick to reassure him. "Never have been. Kissing and cuddling are more than enough for me."

His heart beat a little faster when Niclas nuzzled in closer to him. Grabbing the blanket off the back of the couch, Falk managed to drape it over both of them with a little effort. He smiled when Niclas twisted slightly to rest his head on his chest further.

They woke up in almost the exact same position.

Falk went to stretch, dislodging Niclas and having to grab at him to keep him from falling to the floor. "Morning."

Niclas grabbed Falk's arm and checked his watch. "Oh, sard it. We've slept in. We'll need to be out of here in an hour."

"We'll manage. Packed all my stuff up already. We have to clean up after our late-night snacks. Not much else to do." Falk tried to ease some of Niclas's anxiety. "Why don't you walk me through what you have to do?"

"Might as well do it if I'm walking you through it?"

"I mean talk, Professor Dirt."

"Ah. Right. Of course." Niclas dragged a hand across his face. He yawned so widely that Falk thought he might crack his jaw. "My bags are already packed, so I've got to take them out to my Mini and then do the checklist in the kitchen."

"Checklist?"

"Things the owner of the cottage asks renters to do before they leave." Niclas rolled off the couch to his feet. He stumbled over the carpet but righted himself and went to grab the list. "Make sure the lights are off. Take out the rubbish. And a few other things. I want to have a quick whizz around the bedrooms with the Hoover, make sure we didn't leave a trail of sand in our wake."

"Why don't I fix us up a quick breakfast, then we can take our bags outside?" Falk didn't want Niclas to hold onto his anxiety over leaving on time. They might as well get a move on. "Coffee will do us a world of good."

Even after stopping for showers and breakfast, they managed to leave the cottage a few minutes early. Falk followed Niclas in his vehicle to the next Airbnb in Perranporth. It was larger than Falk expected; all the previous ones had been relatively small in comparison.

It was another converted barn but significantly larger than the last. Five bedrooms, along with a large garden and a conservatory attached to the cottage. It still managed to be cosy and welcoming inside, with vaulted ceilings and a wood-burning stove.

"Think I rattled something loose in my brain driving up the lane." Falk climbed out of his Range Rover to join Niclas, who had already begun to unload his bags from the Mini Cooper. "In a hurry?"

"Still time to drive back up the coast to hit Fistral Beach. It's the first one on this leg of the trip." Niclas struggled with the lockbox near the door, trying to enter the code. Three tries later, he'd managed to get the keys out. Again, he fumbled with the lock before triumphantly pushing open the door. "I hath conquered."

"No door is a match for you." Falk carried his two bags along with the bag of food inside. He whistled at the size of the place. "Were you planning on a large family gathering?"

"They had a last-minute cancellation. So I got a brilliant deal." Niclas dropped his bags by the hallway entrance. "Why don't we pack the food away? I left my gear outside. It's probably an hour to the beach if we hit traffic."

"How about I put this away and grab us snacks? Your water bottle full?"

"No grapes."

"No grapes," Falk promised. He smiled when Niclas snickered to himself. "Maybe we should take you to one of those wineries where they let you stomp on grapes. A little justice."

"Think enough crimes involving grapes have happened in my presence. I don't need to sully my feet in the process." Niclas reached up to stroke his fingers along his throat. "I'm aware of how silly this seems, but I'm subconsciously on edge whenever I eat. As if I'm expecting to choke on another random piece of food."

"Trauma's trauma, whether it comes at the hands of a grape or something else."

"Over a grape?"

Falk set the bag of rubbish down and took Niclas's hand in his own. "Listen, Professor Dirt, you had a moment of terror. You couldn't breathe. That can leave a mark. Just remember to calm yourself. Sip slowly. Chew slowly. After a while, you'll stop panicking whenever you put something in your mouth."

Niclas was silent for a moment. "Will I? Stop panicking whenever I put something in my mouth?"

Falk pressed his lips together before breaking into a grin. He tried desperately not to burst out laughing, given the serious nature of the conversation. "Nic."

Niclas leaned forward, wheezing with laughter. "Good to know."

CHAPTER 17
NICLAS

Laughing with Falk had cleared some of his dark mood. Niclas had slept well on the couch but woken up with the memory of almost choking. He kept obsessing over what had happened; he knew from past experience that it would take time before he forgot.

The drive to Fistral Beach had been pleasant. Falk had lowered the windows, allowing them to enjoy the salty sea air. Blue skies, fluffy clouds, and green fields were all around them, with the glistening sea in the distance. It was almost something out of a movie.

Fistral had a wide swath of beach at low tide with relatively few boulders to navigate around. Niclas hadn't visited before, but he was pleasantly surprised to find it not completely overcrowded with tourists.

They'd timed their visit well. Few tourists to interfere, and no high tide to force him to rush. Falk, once again, found a place to relax while Niclas set his metal detector up. He enjoyed the beaches, but part of him longed to move to the interior.

Underwater detecting was always his favourite. However, he wondered if adjusting his plans would be better. The point of the trip was to enjoy himself, but the beaches had started to feel like a chore.

Halfway through his hunt, crowds increased to the point of making his search complicated. Niclas couldn't really ask people to move out of his way. He finally decided to call it a day after answering what felt like the hundredth question about what he was doing.

Niclas hissed in frustration when another person laid out a blanket on a part of the beach he hadn't scanned yet. *Bampots.* He carried his metal detector over to Falk, who closed his book and got to his feet. "Think I have to reevaluate my plans."

"Oh?" Falk glanced around at the groups of people around them. It was slowly becoming more crowded. "I see your problem. Early mornings then?"

"I'm half tempted to skip more of the beaches and move to the rivers. I enjoy underwater hunting more than this. Quieter. Less likely to have people pestering me with questions." Niclas hated the almost whiny tone of his voice. Next year, he'd try to plan his trip in the off-season for tourists, wherever he chose to go. "I'm ready to depart."

There had always been something charming in the way Niclas spoke. A mixture of forgotten language and turns of phrase. It was uniquely him.

They'd made it to the car park when Niclas noticed a familiar figure heading towards the beach. Charlene spotted him and immediately altered her direction. She smiled prettily at Falk, then narrowed his eyes at Niclas.

"Late in the day to be starting your excursion." Niclas snarked, much to his own surprise. "Trouble with your beauty sleep?"

Charlene seemed as stunned as Falk that Niclas refused to allow things to slide. "Early to be admitting defeat?"

"Defeat?" Niclas set his metal detector down and leaned his arm against the top of it. "Boring word. Mundane. What about kibosh?"

Charlene sniffed. Loudly. Overly loudly. She was going to sneer at him. Niclas hated it now that he realised how she meant it. "I—"

"We're going to fornicate. Goodbye." Niclas ignored Falk's choked laugh and Charlene's aborted sneer. "Enjoy my leftovers. I'm sure there's a crushed can or two left under the sand."

They watched her stomp away towards the beach. Niclas found the adrenaline rush of the confrontation had vanished quickly. He glanced over to find Falk almost red-faced, trying to contain his laughter.

"What?"

"Fornicate?" Falk unlocked the vehicle and put his gear into the back.

"I mean, we aren't. But she doesn't know." Niclas slumped down into the seat of the Range Rover. "I hate change."

"Change?"

Niclas dug his phone out of his backpack. He opened up the app where he scheduled all of the treasure hunts along with his rented cottages. "I technically have a few more beaches on this side of the coast, but thus far, it's all been a dawdle."

"Really?"

"Apart from you." Niclas knew all of his work required patience, from being in the field to the museum. "I'm going to cull through my list of beaches. This won't be my last trip to Cornwall, so I don't have to visit every single one."

"You don't. Cornwall isn't going anywhere."

It wasn't. Niclas spent the rest of the drive back to the cottage, staring at his schedule and considering options. Again. He'd had to evaluate everything multiple times. Change made him anxious.

Itchy and anxious.

When they arrived back at the cottage, Niclas disappeared into his bedroom. He had to take some time to calm down. His confrontation with Charlene, however mild, had taken a lot of his social energy for the day.

Being surrounded by curious tourists hadn't helped either.

It was getting dark when Niclas poked his head out of the bedroom. The weather had cooled off a little. He found Falk in the kitchen, preparing a late supper for them.

"Hungry?" Falk was in the process of making up sandwiches. "Figured something simple would work. We can grab a beer and have these outside. There's a fire pit in the back of the garden. Nice clear, cool summer night. Not a bad end to our day. No grapes were involved in the making of supper."

"Nincompoop," Niclas grumbled. "I'll grab the beers."

"Nincompoop. Not the worst thing I've been

called." Falk finished plating up what he'd made and carried two plates outside. "I'll start the fire."

Checking the bags from the shop on the counter, Niclas found several bags of Roast Beef Monster Munch and a packet of chocolate-covered biscuits. He grabbed both to go with the rest of their meal. Not the healthiest but certainly not the worst of his life.

Niclas stepped outside to find Falk had already started the fire. "All your famed military survival skills coming in handy?"

"Far easier than during training."

"Do you miss it?"

Falk sat back on his heels. He poked at the fire with a stick. "Not really. Not as much as you might think. If I were to miss something, it would be my unit. My friends. And most of them work for my company."

"Do you miss being a medic?"

Falk shifted out of his crouched position into one of the chairs. He stretched his arm out to grab Niclas's chair and dragged it closer to him. "It might be the only part of the work I miss. Then again, you do offer a chance for me to practice those skills more frequently than anticipated."

"Grizz."

"Always good to keep my skills fresh."

"*Grizz.*"

Falk draped his arm across Niclas's shoulders. "Perhaps we can practise mouth-to-mouth resuscitation next?"

CHAPTER 18

FALK

Waking up in bed alone had been a part of Falk's life for a while. He'd dated, but the military then his company had eaten up so much of his time, it hadn't been a priority.

And there'd been the whole matter of being in love with his best friend's younger brother.

Opening his eyes to find a mess of brown hair obscuring his vision had been pleasant. Falk had an arm around Niclas's back. Their legs were tangled together. He vaguely remembered falling asleep together.

The evening had been fun. They'd stoked the fire and talked late into the night. The hints of loneliness that haunted the corners of his heart had vanished with the quiet solace he'd found in Niclas's presence.

"Nic?" Falk kept his voice low. He didn't want to startle Niclas, but his bladder had informed him of a pressing need to get out of bed. "Need you to move?"

Nothing.

"Nic? Professor Dirt?" Falk gently nudged him. He swept a hand down his back, but all Niclas did was shuffle even closer. "I have to get up."

Again, nothing.

"Niclas?" Falk dragged his fingers along Niclas's side and got an immediate reaction.

"Wha—" Niclas raised up a little. His arm flailed over his head, causing his elbow to catch Falk in the face. "Where? What manner of madness—"

"Easy." Falk caught Niclas by the arms to stop his flailing and shifted him onto the mattress. "Are you always so vicious when someone wakes you up?"

"Oh my god." Niclas twisted towards him. He rose up to get a better look at Falk's face. "Your eye. I'm so sorry. So sorry. Oh my god."

"Not the end of the world. I've had worse." Falk could already feel he was going to have a spectacular black eye. "Think there's a bag of peas in the freezer?"

"Oh my god." Niclas covered his face with his hands, hiding the flush on his cheeks. "Don't tell

Izan. He'll never let me forget I punched you in the face."

"Pretty sure he'll approve, since you are in my bed." Falk tried not to laugh, but he couldn't help it. "How's my eye look, professor?"

Niclas refused to pull his hands away from his face. "Oh, the humiliation."

"Hey, hey. It could happen to anyone." Falk tried to sound comforting despite the slight amusement in his voice.

"Yes, but why does it always seem to happen to me?" Niclas sat up and dropped his hands away from his face. He moved up onto his knees to peer into Falk's face. "Well, your eye looks puffy. Not the eye itself. Around it."

Leaning forward even further, Niclas placed a gentle kiss above Falk's eye. He winked at him and then rolled off the bed, muttering about going to find a bag of frozen peas. This had definitely not been the way either of them had planned to start their morning.

Falk flopped back on his pillow and huffed out a laugh. He gingerly touched around his eye, wincing at slight sensitivity. "Never, ever going to live this down if Izan finds out."

Rolling out of bed, Falk snagged his shirt off the floor and pulled it over his head. He stepped into the bathroom and peered in the mirror. A bruise was already beginning to form.

Brilliant.

The only small mercy was Izan had already left. Falk finished up in the bathroom and made his way into the kitchen to find Niclas had gotten distracted from his mission to find frozen peas. Instead, he was messing with the speciality coffee machine in the kitchen.

Niclas spun around when he stepped into the kitchen. He grabbed a bag off the counter and thrust it towards Falk. "Peas? I am most apologetic."

"And I am *mostly* okay." Falk grinned when Niclas leaned up to touch his lips to the corner of his eye. "Miracle cure."

"Have the peas." Niclas pushed the bag into Falk's hand and then lifted both to his eye. "Not how I intended to start our morning."

"You had intentions?"

"Of the vague variety. Holywell Bay. I want to search the dunes. I've done the beach previously." Niclas walked back over to poke at the fancy coffee machine again. "Roman texted me."

"Roman?"

"Not his actual name. Edmund Lloyd. He runs the department that I work for at the museum. He's responsible for all the antiquities being brought in by treasure hunters. Good man. He's in his seventies, and he comes in every morning with his husband, Allan." Niclas rambled for a few more seconds before shaking his head. "Sorry. We call him Roman because he's obsessed with finding specific artefacts dating back to particular Caesars."

"So Roman, not his actual name, texted you?" Falk adjusted the pack of peas on his eye, swiping at the liquid on his cheek. "Everything okay?"

"Charlene called to complain about me." Niclas set two mugs down. He jammed another button on the machine. It beeped, then finally, coffee began flowing —from the nozzle opposite where he'd put the cup. "Oh for…."

There was a second of panicked shuffling before Niclas got the mug in the right spot. He laughed a little hysterically while sopping up the coffee now pooled in front of the machine. Falk grabbed a spare kitchen towel to help.

"So, the river of coffee aside. Charlene complained?"

"Roman laughed off her complaint. She had the audacity to say I was unprofessionally sarcastic. Me? But… me? Not her. Me?" Niclas repeated himself a few times. "Me. I was 'unprofessionally sarcastic.'

On what planet have I ever been more acerbic than her?"

"On planet privileged." Falk had no doubts about how a rich, well-connected, beautiful and clever person might take advantage of many situations. However, Niclas had come into that environment without connections and wealth behind him. "She's not used to you or anyone standing up to her."

"So she tattles on me like we're children?" Niclas grumbled. He yanked open the fridge door and pulled out the fixings to make breakfast. "I'm making my yaya's version of migas."

"Which is?"

"Chorizo, sausage, and bread fried up with an egg on top." Niclas pulled the bread out from the bag they'd brought from the previous cottage. "It's stale enough; it should work."

"Can I help?" Falk went over to wash his hands, joining Niclas by the counter.

They worked side by side, talking through their plans for the day and listening to music Falk queued up on his phone. He had a flash of what a future together might be, but he pushed those thoughts away. It was too soon; the last thing he wanted to do was scare Niclas away.

With breakfast over, they drove out to Holywell

Bay. Niclas wanted to start with the dunes. He hadn't gone over them previously. Falk was happy to just be along for the ride.

"This is my spot."

Niclas didn't stop removing his gear from the boot of the Range Rover when the familiar, grating voice of Charlene interrupted them. "It is not, in fact, your anything. You do not own the Holywell dunes, beach, or bay."

"I'm going to report you." She sounded as if she were seconds away from stamping her foot in frustration.

"For what? Breathing air?" Niclas had clearly reached the end of his rope.

Staying in the background, Falk watched with pride while Niclas stood his ground. He was polite and firm, maybe a little narky. Charlene seemed flummoxed by the change in her self-created adversary.

"I have a permit. This trip was planned ages ago. The museum's acquisitions department head is fully aware of my trip to Cornwall. They're anxiously waiting for any interesting finds." Niclas gripped his detector tightly. "If you don't mind, I'd like to begin while there's still colour in my hair."

With an indignant hiss, Charlene stomped away

from them. Niclas stared after her. He dragged his fingers roughly through his hair.

"You okay?"

"On some level, I'm glad to have stood up for myself, but have I sunk to her level?" Niclas held his headphones up to one ear, testing out the volume. "Ignoring her hasn't worked, but is this better? Izan would say I'm too kind-hearted for my own good. Am I being unprofessional? I'm never quite sure."

"Nothing wrong with being kind-hearted, and I'm confident your brother would agree with me. And no, you didn't cross any lines. You had every right to stand up for yourself." Falk reached up to grab the last of the gear, then closed the lid on the boot. "You're a good sort, Nik. Forget the privileged twits of the world. What do they know?"

"They know a lot of important people and where to get funding for their projects." Niclas slipped his headphones onto his head. "I'm going to start—she'll be back eventually."

"Probably, but there's nothing she can do but throw a tantrum." Falk offered him the flask of tea. "Have a sip. Fortify your nerves. And let's enjoy the beautiful weather."

CHAPTER 19
NICLAS

Niclas sighed, watching Charlene approach for the second time. Finally, he held up a hand to stop her before she could even start. "I have zero interest in this bizarre rivalry you've attempted to cultivate between us."

"Rivalry?" She scoffed.

"I'm here to do a job—and enjoy myself. None of that involves you."

"You wish you were half the—"

"No, I genuinely do not wish I were anything like you at all." Niclas cut her off. He wanted to be done with the conversation and her. "You've harangued me every time you've had the chance. I refuse to placate you further. Leave me alone. Of the two of us, I have a greater cause for reporting you to the

director. Who do you think they're more likely to listen to? Me or you? Considering you've had multiple complaints filed against you. Aren't you on a last warning? Mummy and Daddy's money only goes so far."

"Why you—"

"How about you go find treasure and leave me alone? We're in Cornwall. The weather is cooperating. It's absolutely perfect for metal detecting. Have a good day." Niclas pushed his headphones back on and turned purposefully away from her.

It took an immense amount of self-discipline not to glance in her direction. Niclas focused on the dunes. He breathed a sigh of relief several minutes later when it became clear she'd gone.

A chirping sound disrupted his swirling thoughts about Charlene. Niclas waved the coil across the area several times, honing in on the specific spot before kneeling down and getting to work with his trowel. He carefully dug around the area, ensuring it was large enough to avoid damaging the object.

He expected to find another crushed can, which would make his fifth of the day. "Great Ceasar's ghost."

"You made that one up."

Niclas grinned back at Falk, who'd come to see

what he'd found. "It's nineteenth century, likely connected to Shakespeare."

"Right." Falk didn't seem convinced. "What did you find?"

"Not sure. It's gold, though. I'm 80 percent sure." Niclas handed his detector to Falk while he continued to carefully clear the sand around his find. "Oh, my days."

"Nic?"

"There was a severe summer storm before we arrived with gale-force winds. I wonder if some sand was kicked up at the dunes, making it possible to locate them with my detector." Niclas had no other explanation for how his find had gone undetected. "I'll have to clean them up, but there's a small collection of what I think is jewellery. Maybe some coins. It's hard to tell. From the slivers of wood, I'm guessing they were buried in a chest."

"What exactly have you found?" Falk crouched down beside him. "A hoard?"

"A smallish one." Niclas fished around in his backpack to find the container where he stored new finds. "I can clean these up at the cottage, then I'll have to call the museum. These are definitely going to fall under the Treasure Act. I know the local finds liaison officer. We've worked together a few times, so she'll be as excited as I am."

"Are we heading back to the cottage now?" Falk watched him continue to dig a little, but he failed to find anything else in the hole. "We could grab an early lunch."

"Or late." Niclas put the container away and then took the metal detector. He scanned a few times before deciding he'd definitely found everything. "Can you hold this again?"

Taking his trowel, Niclas put all the sand back. He never left holes open for safety and conservation reasons. It was hard to resist the urge to rush back to the cottage to inspect his finds, but he didn't want to leave the small section of the dunes unscanned.

"I have a little portion of the dunes left to scan." Niclas always disciplined himself not to bail on an area mid-search, if only because the "what-ifs" would drive him mental later on. "I shouldn't take long. I hope."

Not taking long turned into two hours. Niclas found several additional pieces, along with a handful of Roman coins. He thought most, if not all, were from a similar time period. Unfortunately, it was impossible to tell without cleaning and inspecting them.

By the time Niclas finished, he was practically bouncing on his heels. He couldn't contain his excitement. It had been a while since he'd had any major finds.

And this had all the makings of a significant find.

"Hydrate." Falk took the metal detector and backpack out of Niclas's hands, swapping them for a bottle of water. They'd refilled them at the cottage in the morning. "Drink. I was just about to interrupt you for lunch."

"I could eat." Niclas drank slowly. He was still a little paranoid about chugging liquids after his experience with the grape.

Falk dug into the pack that he carried for a packet of crisps. "Here. Have a snack to tide you over until we get back to the cottage."

The drive to the cottage seemed to take forever. All Niclas wanted to do was inspect all of his finds. Thoughts swirled around in his mind at what the small collection of items might contain.

Once they were on the road, Niclas pulled out his phone to text Deidre. She handled treasure finds in Cornwall. They'd worked together many times in the past.

She told him to message photos once his finds were cleaned up. Her office was thirty minutes away, so she invited them for lunch to go over them in person the next day. There were a lot of exclamation points in her text.

Once at the cottage, Niclas practically ran inside with his backpack. He paused to set the metal detector by the door. It took a second for him to grab his container and move to the kitchen.

Spreading paper on the kitchen table, Niclas placed the container on top. He dug into his bag for his toolkit. He filled a bowl with water to help with cleaning the artefacts.

His mind calmed while he reverently removed each item from the container. He lined them all up on the paper. It was the second most significant find of his career.

"While you work, how about I go into the village and pick something up to eat? Any special requests to celebrate your find?" Falk came over to stand behind him. He gripped him lightly by the shoulders and bent down to kiss the top of his head. "Anything at all?"

"Chips with curry sauce."

"Not exactly a full meal."

"You said anything." Niclas tilted his head back to smile at Falk. "Chips with curry sauce. Extra chips. I wouldn't say no to a piece of fish."

Falk chuckled above him before leaning in for

another kiss. "Chips with a side of fish, coming right up."

"Extra chips."

"I will not forget the extra while I forage for chips." Falk dipped down for one final kiss before heading towards the door. "Don't eat any grapes while I'm gone."

"Droll. Very, very droll."

Counting out a few breaths until his heart rate slowed to a normal pace, Niclas reached for the coins first. The least exciting part of his find. He carefully cleaned them off, took photos, and stored them in a separate container.

Niclas grabbed his notebook. He opened to a new page, notating the date at the top and creating a detailed log of the coins. *Not bad, not bad.*

Most of the coins were some sort of copper alloy and badly corroded. He didn't know if the museum would wind up wanting them. But the gold and silver coins were in fantastic condition.

Setting his notebook to one side, Niclas mentally categorised all the remaining items. He wanted to get a better look at the ring, but some of the other pieces of jewellery intrigued him. What was underneath thousands of years of mud, sand, and corrosion? What little part of history had he potentially found?

Since Niclas had already partially identified the ring, he first focused on the other artefacts. He picked up what appeared to be a pendant or maybe an earring. It was hard to tell with all the sand caked around it.

Niclas grabbed one of the smaller brushes. He held the delicate piece and began the meticulous work of cleaning it off. "There you are. Aren't you lovely?"

There was only a single earring. He hadn't found the matching one. It was gold. A long delicate piece with an inverted drop-shaped ornament at the bottom with braided wire and flowers making up the top. The design reminded him of second-century AD ones he'd seen in a museum catalogue a few years ago.

Once Niclas had cleaned the earring off, he gently placed it into a container. He went for the necklace next. It had been crushed at some point; the gold torque was more of a flat line than a stiff ring.

The necklace itself was made up of eight gold ropes twisted together. Only one of the ends remained; the other had been broken off at some point. It was an intricately designed lion head. It was a shame part had been destroyed.

Still, even with just one of the lion heads, it made for a fantastic addition to his small hoard, as would the simple gold bracelets. He'd found three of them.

One was tiny enough that it had probably been meant for a child.

Niclas worked through each item until he finally picked up the ring. "Ah. Pièce de résistance. What secrets are you going to reveal to me?"

CHAPTER 20
FALK

Falk picked up a few pastries from a bakery next to the chippie to go with the massive mound of curry chips and fish. Something sweet to celebrate the find. He took his time, hoping to give Niclas time to inspect everything on his own without someone peering over his shoulder.

It also gave him time to check out some of the other shops. Falk returned to the cottage after a few hours, hopefully having given Niclas enough time to himself. It was almost eerily quiet.

"Nic?" Falk carried the multiple bags through to find Niclas carefully inspecting a ring. "You okay, Professor Dirt?"

"What?" Niclas bolted upright. He flung a hand

out to grab a bottle of water. "Oh, my days. You startled me. This intaglio ring is perfection."

"Sorry. Here we have a shed-load of chips and an ocean of curry." Falk set the hefty bag on the kitchen counter. "Only a mild exaggeration."

"Smells divine." Niclas flushed when his stomach growled loudly. "I am apparently hungry."

"Why don't we eat outside by the firepit? Enjoy the fading sunlight and the outdoors. You can leave all your artefacts on the kitchen table." Falk pulled the containers of food out of the bag and set them on the counter. He grabbed two plates for them. "Not a bad life to have."

"Pardon?"

"This. Us. Travelling. You finding treasure. Enjoying sunsets while we share a meal." Falk dumped a portion of the chips onto a plate along with two pieces of fish. "I could do this forever."

"Is it too early for the forever kind of talk?"

"How long have we been in love with each other but too afraid to say something?" Falk knew the answer for himself. Too long. They'd thrown away so many opportunities because of fear and self-doubt.

Niclas glanced briefly up into his eyes, then back down to the ring in his hands. He swallowed loudly, clearing his throat before finally speaking. "A lifetime."

"How many of those do we have to waste?"

"None. We've certainly wasted enough time, mine own hertis rote." Niclas carefully secured the ring before coming to stand beside Falk.

"Hertis road?"

"Rote. Middle English. Myne owne hertis rote." Niclas placed a hand over his heart and then reached out with his other to rest against Falk's chest. "My own heart's root would be the direct translation. You're the very depth of my soul."

Falk reached up to cover his hand, pulling him forward and tilting his head until their lips met. "Think we're done wasting time, Nic."

Niclas went to respond, but his stomach grumbled loudly for a second time. "Right. So… chips?"

"Chips."

Gathering up their plates, they made their way outside. The sun was just beginning to set. Falk got a fire going once again. He hadn't been exaggerating; he could happily spend the rest of his life travelling with Niclas.

"Tell me about your finds. What exactly is an intaglio ring?" Falk grabbed his little wooden fork and began eating his fish.

"The engraved stone—an amethyst in this case. It works as a seal. That's why it's called an intaglio ring." Niclas dragged a chip through the curry before popping it into his mouth. "The recessed image was carved into the gem. Mostly wealthy businessmen and politicians had them. They'd be pressed into hot wax as a signature."

"You have a wealth of knowledge."

"About very specific and obscure subjects." Niclas licked curry off his fingers. He slumped down into the seat with a satisfied sigh.

"How serious of a find is your hoard?"

"Not sure it strictly qualifies as a hoard. Not large enough for the classification. We'll see." Niclas waved a chip around, sending curry flying everywhere. "Similar ring auctioned off in a private sale a few years ago for around forty thousand."

"For one ring?"

"One quite ancient ring with some measure of historical significance. I haven't gotten a close enough look at this one yet. If I can identify the original owner, it might be worth quite a lot. The seal might be the key, if it's unique." Niclas grabbed the last of his chips. "That is a project for after my summer travels."

"What do your instincts say?"

"I'll be able to age the ring but not find the owner." Niclas shrugged. He inspected the packet before crushing it and slipping it into the bag. "Not all that unusual for ancient artefacts of this type. Some of the symbols were quite commonplace."

"So you've found something extraordinarily ordinary." Falk grinned when Niclas scowled at his nose. He could always tell where Niclas had chosen to direct his gaze.

"Did you mean what you said earlier? About travelling together? Being… together?"

"With every root of my heart." Falk frowned, then laughed at himself. "Sounded far more romantic when you said it."

"I have the oddest vision of tree roots sprouting out of your heart." Niclas took a sip out of his drink. "Might make an interesting tattoo."

"Not a bad idea."

"Being poked a million times by a need seems like the worst possible idea." Niclas accepted the packet of chips from Falk, who'd had a few left over. "Are we dating? Are you my boyfriend?"

"I'm apparently your hertis rote." Falk grinned when Niclas rolled his eyes and sighed dramatically. "Am I not? What would you say we are?"

"We're…."

"Undefinable?"

Niclas picked up one of the chips, dragging it through the curry. "Fairly confident I could find a word if I tried hard enough."

Late in the evening, Falk had just gotten into bed when a soft knock drew his attention. A pyjama-clad Niclas poked his head into the room. He came all the way in a second later.

"Something wrong?"

"I've enjoyed our time in the evenings." Niclas hesitated by the door. He took a few deep breaths, then came over to stand by the bed and reached down to rest his fingers against the edge of the duvet. "And I can't seem to drift off into the ether."

Falk lifted up the duvet and patted the empty space beside him. "Hop in."

There was another moment of hesitation before Niclas joined him. He slid under the duvet. They lay side by side on their backs for several awkward minutes.

Falk rolled over on his side. He reached out to drag Niclas closer and was surprised when he burrowed in and wrapped his arms around him tightly. "Am I just an oversized teddy bear for you to cuddle with?"

"May you have the sweetest of dreams, Grizz."

Niclas's laugh was cut off by a yawn. "You're not the softest of bears."

"Good night, Nic."

THE NEXT FEW WEEKS FLEW BY IN SEEMED LIKE THE blink of an eye. Falk had enjoyed himself immensely with Niclas. Jess had teased him about "having a honeymoon without all the faff of a ceremony" and then couriered a wedding cake to them as a joke.

They'd enjoyed the cake, but Niclas had been rather confused. Falk decided not to mention honeymoons and marriages. No matter how much everyone at his company seemed to take pleasure in nudging him in jest about it.

They were heading to the last Airbnb of the journey, a lovely little cottage outside of Liskeard. Niclas intended to spend the rest of his time along the River Lynher and several of its tributaries before finally heading home.

None of the locations after Holywell Bay had turned up anything more exciting than a buckle and a few buttons. Niclas didn't appear bothered. He attacked each beach or river with the same excited fervour, driven to find any sliver of history buried in the ground.

The weeks had given Falk plenty of time to consider the future. His. And theirs. They were changes he hoped to make once this extended vacation ended. Things that he wanted to talk to Niclas about eventually, but not yet.

Not until he'd worked things out completely.

CHAPTER 21
NICLAS

IT HAD BEEN THE BEST TREASURE-HUNTING TRIP OF his career thus far. Niclas found it difficult to believe there was only a week left. He was usually more than ready to be finished by this point.

He *usually* longed for his own bed and the quiet of his home.

Usually.

But Falk had changed everything. Niclas found himself not wanting the idyllic summer to be over. It hadn't been perfect, nothing in life was, but it had been the closest he'd ever experienced.

"Morning." Falk rolled over in bed. His arm draped heavily across Niclas's chest. "Thinking heavy thoughts for however early it is in the morning."

"We're moving on to the last river." Niclas tried to

figure out how to put into words the doubts rolling around in his mind. It had kept him up half the night. "What happens next?"

"Showers? Breakfast? You diving in a mucky river?" Falk teased. He shifted further onto his side. "What's going on?"

"What happens when I head home?"

"What do you want to happen?" Falk sat up with his back against a pillow, pulling Niclas up to join him. "I'm hoping this wasn't just a summer fling."

"Don't be a nincompoop." Niclas elbowed him lightly in the side. He liked the weight of Falk's arm across his shoulders, drawing him closer. It was more comforting than the weighted blanket Izan had gotten for him a few years ago. "Roman emailed me yester-day. He's been speaking with his friend who runs the acquisitions department at the museum in Truro. They've an opening for someone to handle, process, and research incoming finds." Niclas had been thrilled and terrified by the offer. "So, I might be moving to Cornwall. They've given me a few days to make my decision. They're even offering a bonus to help with any expenses in the move. I'd start at the end of the month."

"It would be a lovely life. A little cottage in Corn-wall." Falk smiled when Niclas whipped his head around to glance at him. "One of the perks of running my own business, particularly one like mine, is I can work from anywhere. Half of the employees tend to work from home. We only have the office for all the admin nonsense. Don't tell anyone I called them that."

"Your secret is safe with me." Niclas tilted his head to rest against Falk's shoulder. "What are you saying? I'm loath to move the conversation forward without having a clear idea of what you're trying to tell me. I'm… not gifted at deciphering all the things non-autistics say between the lines."

"The longer this summer has gone on, the more I've dreaded the end of our adventure because I assumed it meant seeing less of you." Falk voiced the same fear Niclas had been harbouring in his heart. "I'm not itching to be done with you."

"Always found that to be the oddest turn of phrase. How exactly do you itch to do something? Don't answer. Purely rhetorical." Niclas tried to stop his mind from swirling around like a whirling dervish. It often felt like his brain might careen out of his control. "Would you… Am I ridiculous for asking if you'd consider moving with me to Truro? Or somewhere close by?"

"You're not ridiculous." Falk sat both of them up,

twisting around so they were facing each other. "This conversation has devolved into a stilted and painfully awkward thing."

Niclas sighed in relief. He'd thought he was the only one feeling almost constrained. "Maybe it's too soon, but Izan always says you learn more about someone when you're travelling and living with them than you do any other time. And I've known you forever."

"Been in love forever?"

"Almost forever." Niclas grinned. He felt a giddiness bubbling up inside of him. "I'm taking the position. It's a brilliant leap in my career. I'd practically be in charge of my own team. And I love Cornwall. Would you be interested in moving with me?"

"I would."

"Genuinely?" Niclas had expected him to say no or maybe. He hadn't expected an immediate yes. "Are you sure?"

"I'm the boss. My company has done far better than any of us ever imagined. I can work from anywhere. Cornwall's not half bad, especially with you here." Falk chuckled, letting Niclas know he was teasing. "Why don't we take it a step at a time?"

"Step one?"

"A warm mug of tea and some toast. We can sit in

the garden and contemplate the future." Falk reached out to run his fingers through Niclas's messy hair. "Everything always seems calmer and clearer after caffeine."

"Not coffee?"

"Maybe later. Tea, first." Falk drew him in for a slow, languid kiss, then pulled back with another laugh. "Tea and toast."

They meandered into the kitchen. Niclas slumped against the counter, staring at the kettle to make it boil faster. Falk handled getting bread into the toaster.

"What are we having with our toast?" Falk nudged his elbow when he didn't answer. "You with me, Professor Dirt?"

"Partially." Niclas had to force his eyes open. "I couldn't drop off last night. I kept thinking about all changes that are about to happen. Am I even qualified for the position?"

"You're the cleverest person I've ever met. So dedicated. So patient. How many years have you worked to archive and study the treasures found?" Falk sounded so confident. "You can do this, Nic. No doubt in my mind."

Not trusting his voice, Niclas nodded. He focused on getting their tea ready while Falk finished with the toast. They carried their breakfast outside.

"Breakfast in the garden? We are lords of leisure." Niclas hadn't bothered to change out of his pyjamas. His feet were bare. They'd slept in longer than usual, so it wasn't too cold. He enjoyed the feeling of the soft grass against his toes. "I don't even know what our next steps should be."

"One of my employees has a sister who works as an estate agent in Truro. How about I reach out? Maybe they can put together a list of properties within our price range?" Falk sipped his tea. He stretched his legs out and relaxed into the chair. "We'll go halves. Joint owners."

"Falk."

"However we choose to define our relationship, I want us to always be equal partners." Falk didn't back down until Niclas nodded his agreement. "I've seen things fall apart when people don't feel respected and equal with the person they love."

"Is this a snapshot of our future?"

"We'll have a better garden." Falk stretched his arm out to knock his mug against Niclas's. "To the future."

"A future without grapes."

Falk laughed with him for a second. "To our future together with love and no grapes."

It seemed almost too good to be true for Niclas.

He'd never imagined a future with Falk, when he'd been admiring him from afar for so long. Could they really have a happy ending?

"Love and no grapes." Niclas nodded his agreement.

CHAPTER 22
FALK

"WHEN ARE YOU GOING TO MAKE AN HONEST MAN out of my little brother, Grizz?" Izan teased while they worked together in the cottage garden. They were building an insulated garden shed as a birthday present for Niclas. "Seriously. Have you thought about it?"

"Iz." Falk had fielded pointed questions from his best friend for a few months. He stopped him from continuing with a sharper tone than usual, drawing a glance from Izan. "We're happy. Quit putting pressure on us."

"I'm joking."

"Don't." Falk was pricklier than normal. He turned away from Izan, whose sharp eyes had narrowed. "Why don't—"

"You're going to propose." Izan gestured with the spirit level in his hand towards the shed. "That's why you wanted to build this while he went on his trip to Greece. So? What's the plan?"

"I'll tell you afterwards."

The past year had been a brilliant roller-coaster ride. Falk had never been happier. They'd both found life together was everything they'd ever imagined.

It had taken a month to find the perfect cottage. Finally, they'd chosen a two-bedroom, two-bath home. It was on the banks of a river with a large garden and stunning views on all sides.

While the cottage was old, the interior had been recently renovated and modernised. They'd turned the second bedroom into an office for Falk. It was part of the reason he'd wanted to build a decent-sized, insulated shed for Niclas to use as a workshop.

Niclas had fallen in love with his new position. There were no Charlenes to make his life miserable. His confidence in his abilities had increased with each month; watching him flourish was wonderful.

"Earth to Falk. You still with me?" Izan drew him out of his thoughts. "Am I building this myself?"

They spent a week working on the insulated shed. Izan left a few days before Niclas's return. A client issue had required him to head to London; Falk had taken a step back from the daily management of the company.

Retired without actually retiring.

"Penny for your thoughts?" Niclas had come home tired and excited about his travels.

"Have you thought about scanning the garden before we make any changes?" Falk hadn't shown him the shed yet. "You never know what you might find."

"What've you done?" Niclas eyed him suspiciously. "And why was Izan here? I saw a pair of his socks under the coffee table."

"Of course you did." Falk drew Niclas into a hug. He twisted them around and guided him toward the back door that led out into the garden. "Close your eyes."

"Is that wise? I stumble at least once a day with both eyes open." Niclas laughed when Falk brought his hands up to cover his eyes. "Fine, fine. On your head be it."

They managed to get out into the garden safely. Falk dropped his hands away, revealing the shed with large, double-glazed windows and french doors. The outer panels were painted a slate grey, while the interior was white with pops of colour here and there.

"What's all this?"

"I made you an office. Your brother helped a little. He was mostly a nuisance. This is somewhere you can go when you need to be alone with your artefacts." Falk kept a light tone to his voice. He knew Niclas had days where he required space to allow himself to recover. "There's space for all your equipment. A desk. Some shelves. We had help with some of the décor."

"You said décor like it was an alien entity." Niclas carefully inspected the entire shed. He froze when he spotted the metal detector leaning up against the corner behind the desk. "You didn't…"

"I thought you might want something new to scan the backyard." Falk barely had time to catch the bag Niclas tossed in his direction. "Now?"

"New. Shiny. Equipment." Niclas drew out each word while admiring his new metal detector. "Oh, I'm so excited."

Without even waiting for a response, Niclas was out in the garden with his new detector. He'd taken barely a few minutes to get it set up. Falk could only watch in amused silence while he immediately started scanning the first patch of the garden.

"I found something."

Falk frowned when he realized Niclas wasn't

anywhere close to where he'd buried the two rings. *What?* "Have you?"

Niclas darted into his new office to find his tools. He was back in seconds, kneeling in the dirt and digging up a hole. "Oh my days, I found a ring."

"Have you?" Falk repeated himself.

Niclas sat back on his heels. He pulled the brush off his tool belt and gently cleaned it enough for a closer look. "Think this might be Tudor era."

"What—" Falk stared at him dumbfounded. "Maybe you should keep searching? There might be something else?"

Niclas narrowed his eyes at Falk. "You are suspiciously excited about my scanning the garden. Why?"

"No reason."

"Okay. Why don't you point me in a direction to scan?" Niclas waved the detector around in a slow circle. "To the right? Left?"

"I don't know what you're talking about."

"Codswallop." Niclas grinned at him. He ran the detector over Falk's shoes. "Here?"

With a sign of resignation, Falk gestured in the general direction of where he'd hidden the rings. It would still be a surprise. Niclas had no idea what he'd buried in the garden.

To his utter amusement and amazement, they had

even more false starts. Falk was beginning to doubt himself. Had he even buried the rings at all?

"Guessing this isn't it?" Niclas held up a crushed can. He snickered when Falk groaned. "I'll keep going."

Ten minutes later, Falk was beginning to give up. Were they ever going to find the rings? It had seemed like such a good idea when he'd come up with it.

Note to self: never, ever mention this part to Izan.

He'll never let us live it down.

A pinging caught his attention. Niclas waved the detector over the same spot a few times before setting it to one side. Then, he knelt down once again with his handy trowel to dig another hole in their garden.

Falk held his breath while waiting to see what he'd discovered this time. "Another can?"

"What—" Niclas sat back on his heels. He had two dirt-covered rings in his hand. His fingers trembled while he cleaned them up. "Myne owne hertis rote."

"I had them engraved to make them ours." Falk knelt in front of him, ignoring the wet grass and mud pushing against his jeans. "Something occurred to me while you were gone."

"Oh?" Niclas couldn't tear his gaze away from the

rings. His finger traced the engraving on the inside of one of them. "I don't…"

"I've wasted so much time loving you from a distance." Falk plucked the smaller of the two rings out of Niclas's hand. "I want there to be a tangible representation of our feelings."

"Falk."

"You're brilliant. Incandescent. You make me laugh. I want everyone to know I'm yours." Falk held the ring up between his fingers. He'd spent a ridiculously long time trying to find the perfect ones before settling on a plain band. The engraving mattered more. Those words. They cut through all the flowery talk he'd practised in the mirror—something he'd never admit to anyone. "Will you marry me?"

"You want *everyone* to know? Everyone in the world?"

"Hyperbole." Falk had to laugh at how his vision for a deeply romantic moment had gone sideways in such a classic them way. "Also, not actually the point of my declaration. Will you marry me?"

The silence stretched on for what seemed like forever. Falk watched Niclas's gaze flicked between the rings, then back at him. Had he actually misjudged the moment?

He couldn't say no. Could he? Falk felt a wave of nervousness hit him unexpectedly.

"Nic?"

"When we tell this story? How about we leave out the fact that I found two crushed cans, a Tudor ring, and a belt buckle from the seventies?" Niclas huffed out an embarrassed chuckle while Falk waited patiently for an answer to his question. "Why do you keep staring at me?"

"You haven't actually said yes."

"Ah. Right. Well, yes. Obviously." Niclas had never seemed to struggle for words aside from when he needed quiet time. He was adorably flustered. "That Tudor ring could be worth a quarter of a million."

"And?"

Niclas lifted up the simple gold band in his hand. "This is infinitely more precious and valuable."

"It is."

Niclas grabbed Falk's hand. He jammed the ring onto Falk's finger a little roughly, causing it to get caught on his knuckle. "Sard it. Why am I always so rubbish with this?"

"You often get engaged? Easy there, Professor Dirt. The ring, the finger, and the proposal aren't going anywhere." Falk grinned when Niclas closed his eyes and muttered under his breath. He peered down at the now scraped knuckle. "Sealed in blood?"

"Don't be macabre." Niclas watched him suck on his knuckle for a second to stem the flow of blood.

"You drew blood." Falk couldn't help bursting out laughing. They were kneeling in the mud and grass of the garden. It had started to drizzle. They were holding engagement bands, and his knuckle was bleeding. "Can I have your hand?"

Niclas lifted his hand up, trying to control his own laughter. "With this ring, I thee wed?"

"Have you said yes yet?"

Falk glanced behind them to see Izan looking over the fence. "What the—"

"I decided to come back and see if my little brother took pity on an old grizzly bear." Izan showed absolutely no shame while stepping into their romantic moment. "Well? Am I scrounging around for a plus one to a stunning wedding on a remote Cornish beach?"

Falk surrendered to the inevitable. He got to his feet and pulled Niclas up with him. "I say this with all the love and care in my heart. Bugger off."

"Fine way to treat your best friend and future brother-in-law, considering I brought you a takeaway for an early supper." Izan handed Falk the bag that he'd been hiding behind his back. He pulled Niclas into a hug. "Congratulations, Professor. Don't let Grizz eat all the chips."

"Want to join us?" Niclas's invite sounded half-hearted to all of them, making both Izan and Falk snicker. "I am mostly sincere."

"Mostly or most?" Izan teased his younger brother. He ruffled his hair, then released him from his hug. "I'm heading home. Don't elope."

The light drizzle began to turn into a proper summer storm. Niclas rushed to take his new detector and finds into his office. They shut the doors and dashed across the garden into the safety of the cottage to enjoy their supper.

Setting the bag of food on the little kitchen table, Niclas leaned against the counter. He twisted the ring on his finger, his attention focused solely on it.

Falk strode over to him, gripping the edge of the counter on either side. He canted his head to the side and leaned in for a kiss. "I love you."

"Pleased to hear it, considering we're betrothed. Affianced." Niclas smiled into the kiss and pulled back. "A year ago, you were a dream just out of reach. A fleeting thought that vanished whenever I opened my eyes."

"And now?"

Niclas tilted his head up for another kiss. "Amidst the hundred stubbed toes and dating woes that befell us over the course of the year, I'm blissfully happy in a way I never imagined possible."

"You're saying I've kissed it better?" Falk couldn't help teasing.

"Maybe we should go for one more—just to ensure I'm fully cured."

Falk answered his smile with a grin of his own. "I do believe in being thorough when it comes to love, kisses, and healing stubbed toes."

ARE YOU READY TO FALL OFF THE PITCH AND INTO love? You can do so in my international bestselling gay romance series, The Sin Bin. Each book features hot rugby players and the men who steal their hearts. Start the series today with THE WANDERER.

Needing more sweetness, hilarious antics, and a stand-alone? Why not check out PURE DUMB LUCK? When two small-town country dudes win the lottery, they finally find the courage to speak their truth. An unexpected adventure follows.

ACKNOWLEDGMENTS

A massive thank-you to my brilliant betas who take my first draft and help me turn it into something legible. To Becky, Olivia, and all the fantastic people at Tangled Tree and Hot Tree Publishing. And also to my beloved hubby, who keeps me from losing my mind while I'm stressing over word counts.

And, lastly, thank you, readers, for following me on my writing journey. I hope you enjoyed *Stubbed Toes & Dating Woes*.

ABOUT THE AUTHOR

Dahlia Donovan wrote her first romance series after a crazy dream about shifters and damsels in distress. She prefers irreverent humour and unconventional characters. An autistic and occasional hermit, her life wouldn't be complete without her husband and her massive collection of books and video games.

Join Dahlia's newsletter: HTTP://EEPURL.COM/Q0N0X

Dahlia would love to hear from you directly, too. Please feel free to email her at DAHLIA@DAHLIADONO-VAN.COM or check out her website DAHLIADONO-VAN.COM for updates.

facebook.com/dahliadonovan

twitter.com/DahliaDonovan

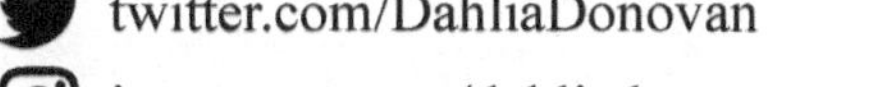
instagram.com/dahliadonovanauthor

bookbub.com/authors/dahlia-donovan

ABOUT THE PUBLISHER

Hot Tree Publishing loves love. Publishing adult romantic fiction, HTPubs are all about diverse reads featuring heroes and heroines to swoon over. Since opening in 2015, HTPubs have published more than 300 titles across the wide and diverse range of romantic genres. If you're chasing a happily ever after in your favourite subgenre, HTPubs have you covered.

Interested in discovering more amazing reads brought to you by Hot Tree Publishing? Head over to the website for information:

WWW.HOTTREEPUBLISHING.COM

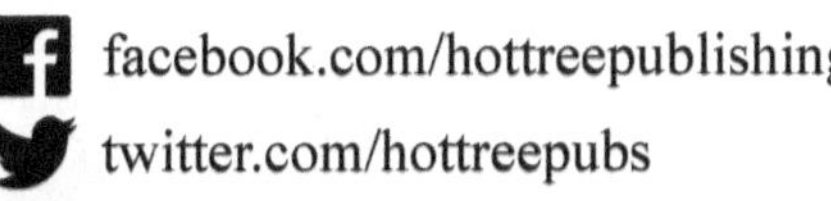